SO THEY DON'T HAVE TO

A Delta Force Unleashed Thriller

Also by J. Robert Kennedy

James Acton Thrillers

The Protocol
Brass Monkey
Broken Dove
The Templar's Relic
Flags of Sin
The Arab Fall
The Circle of Eight
The Venice Code
Pompeii's Ghosts
Amazon Burning
The Riddle
Blood Relics
Sins of the Titanic

Saint Peter's Soldiers
The Thirteenth Legion
Raging Sun
Wages of Sin
Wrath of the Gods
The Templar's Revenge
The Nazi's Engineer
Atlantis Lost
The Cylon Curse
The Viking Deception
Keepers of the Lost Ark
The Tomb of Genghis Khan
The Manila Deception
The Fourth Bible

Embassy of the Empire
Armageddon
No Good Deed
The Last Soviet
Lake of Bones
Fatal Reunion
The Resurrection Tablet
The Antarctica Incident
The Ghosts of Paris
No More Secrets
The Curse of Imhotep
The Heretics Bible
The Hunt for the Holy Grail

Dylan Kane Thrillers

Rogue Operator
Containment Failure
Cold Warriors
Death to America
Black Widow

The Agenda
Retribution
State Sanctioned
Extraordinary Rendition
Red Eagle

The Messenger
The Defector
The Mole
The Arsenal
The Betrayal

Just Jack Thrillers

You Don't Know Jack

Jack Be Nimble

Templar Detective Thrillers

The Templar Detective
The Parisian Adulteress
The Sergeant's Secret

The Unholy Exorcist
The Code Breaker

The Black Scourge
The Lost Children
The Satanic Whisper

Kriminalinspektor Wolfgang Vogel Mysteries

The Colonel's Wife

Sins of the Child

Delta Force Unleashed Thrillers

Payback
Infidels
The Lazarus Moment
Kill Chain

Forgotten
The Cuban Incident
Rampage
Inside the Wire

Charlie Foxtrot
A Price Too High
Righteous Hell
So They Don't Have To

Detective Shakespeare Mysteries

Depraved Difference

Tick Tock

The Redeemer

Zander Varga, Vampire Detective

The Turned

SO THEY DON'T HAVE TO

A Delta Force Unleashed Thriller

J. ROBERT KENNEDY

This is a work of fiction. Names, characters, places, and incidents are products of the author's imagination. Any resemblance to actual persons, living or dead, is entirely coincidental.

ISBN: 9781998005956

First Edition

For Maricris,
who brought me peace.

SO THEY

DON'T HAVE TO

A Delta Force Unleashed Thriller

"It was a perfectly beautiful night, as fall nights are in Washington. I walked out of the Oval Office, and as I walked out, I thought I might never live to see another Saturday night."

Secretary of Defense Robert S. McNamara, recalling the Cuban Missile Crisis
November 1998

"The situation in Venezuela continues to pose an unusual and extraordinary threat to the national security and foreign policy of the United States."

President Joe Biden
March 1, 2023

PREFACE

Venezuela was once one of Latin America's wealthiest nations thanks to vast oil reserves discovered in the early twentieth century. At one time the world's largest exporter of oil, its economy became dependent on it, and declining prices led to a debt and inflation crisis.

In 1998, Hugo Chávez was elected, and his socialist policies led to further decline, with foreign investment fleeing the country after industries were nationalized. Upon his death in 2013, Nicolás Maduro took power, and things have declined even further, with inflation peaking in February 2019 at 344,509.50%. Poverty is rampant, and the latest elections, where the people prayed hope might be restored, have widely been condemned as rigged, with the likely true winner forced to seek asylum in Spain rather than face arrest by the corrupt regime.

Maduro's "victory" was recognized by such fine states as Russia, China, Iran, North Korea and Cuba, and with Venezuela's continued troubles, and open hostility toward the United States and its Western allies, it is perhaps inevitable that our enemies would take interest in this nearly failed state, and take advantage, threatening the power dynamic in the entire hemisphere.

And requiring a swift and effective response.

SEBIN Black Site

Bolivarian Republic of Venezuela

Sergeant Carl "Niner" Sung surged down the steps, his suppressed-M4 raised high. The din of the mayhem outside quickly faded as he rounded a corner, the damp concrete walls flanking a long corridor stretching before him, exactly as described by their contact. The walls were lined with metal doors, each cell potentially holding a prisoner. One of them, hopefully, was their target.

The power was out, leaving two dim, battery-operated lights barely illuminating the passage. Something moved ahead. He squeezed the trigger twice, taking out a member of the Venezuelan secret police. They were famously brutal, unforgiving, and indifferent to human rights. There was no room for mercy in their playbook, and he prayed they weren't too late. Their target had been in enemy hands for almost two days—plenty of time to do serious damage.

Sergeant Leon "Atlas" James shadowed him, followed closely by Command Sergeant Major Burt "Big Dog" Dawson.

"Corporal Diego Mendoza! Identify yourself!" shouted Dawson.

Niner smirked.

They know we're here now.

Their team lead had made the right call. There wasn't time to search every cell. Pounding on a door to his left confirmed Dawson's strategy had worked. Niner pressed forward toward the far end of the corridor where they had been told a set of stairs led up into the lone building on the compound. Any resistance would come from there.

More movement ahead. He adjusted his aim and waited to take the shot. Behind him, a cell door swung open and Dawson ordered their target to leave the way they had come. The hostile ahead poked his head out and Niner fired, dropping the man.

"Fall back! We've retrieved the target!" commanded Dawson.

Niner immediately halted his advance, backing up. He sensed Atlas on his left flank, slightly behind him, when something caught his eye in the dim light. A metallic object clanged against the concrete—a sound both distinctive and terrifying.

"Grenade!" he shouted as he rushed forward, booting the small ball of destruction back toward its source. But it was too late. The explosion, at ceiling level thanks to his quick thinking, tore through the confined corridor. The shockwave slammed him into the ground, debris pummeling his body from overhead, and a strange sensation overtook him as his rapidly beating heart suddenly fell silent in his ears.

It was almost anticlimactic as his life flashed before his eyes— challenges, failures, loves, and broken hearts, the smile of his best friend the last thing he saw before everything went dark.

Leaving a life incomplete, because some idiot had decided to travel to Venezuela.

El Consejo, Venezuela

Two days earlier

"Close your eyes."

Valeria Rojas eyed her American cousin, Diego Mendoza. "Why?"

"I have a surprise for you."

Normally, she wouldn't trust anyone with such a demand, especially someone she barely knew. But she trusted Diego. After all, he was American. And a relative.

"Fine." She closed her eyes.

"Open your mouth."

"What?"

"Just open your mouth."

She groaned. "Fine, but—." Something was stuck in her mouth, cutting her off.

"Bite down."

She did. It was slightly crunchy, but soft as well.

"Now chew."

She complied. Her eyes shot wide as she smiled, continuing to chew. It was delicious, as sweet as anything she had ever tasted. "What is it?"

"It's a candy bar."

She gave him a look. "I figured that out myself. I'm not an idiot. What kind?"

He held up a small wrapper. "KitKat. My personal favorite."

She continued to chew. "So good!"

"You've never had a candy bar before?"

She thought about it as she took the second half from her cousin. "Maybe once or twice. Everything's so expensive. Dad hasn't been able to get a good price for his crops for years. Things are tough here."

Diego frowned, squeezing her shoulder. "I know. I thought things were tough back home. I had no idea how bad it was here. I heard stories, of course, but I had no idea it had gotten so bad."

They continued to stroll toward the market, the sun warm on her face, the muscles in her cheeks sore from so much smiling. "How old were you when you left?"

"I guess I was about your age. Twelve or thirteen."

"Why did you leave?"

"It was tough. My father, your uncle, was arrested. Our neighbor accused him of conspiring against the government."

Her eyes shot wide. "Was he?"

"No, it was a dispute over who should pay for a fence. Back then, all you had to do was accuse someone of being against the government. That was enough to get them out of your life for a while."

She scowled. "It's still the same."

"Well, my father was arrested, so my mother took me and everything we could carry, and we headed north. We traveled through Central America and Mexico. We applied for entry into the United States as political refugees, and we were eventually accepted."

"One day, I'd like to live in America."

He smiled down at her. "Well, if you make it, you'll always have a place to stay."

Her heart leaped. "You would let me stay with you?"

"Of course. You're family. Family is everything."

Goosebumps rippled across her body. She had wanted to go to America for as long as she could remember—to escape the hell that was her home. Her grandparents talked of a Venezuela that was so much better, freer, less oppressive. But that was long gone.

Her country was now a hellhole. Not that she had anything to compare it to beyond the stories she heard, the America she saw on TV, or the rare movie she might be lucky enough to see. It seemed like such an amazing place. A place where you didn't worry about the police knocking down your door, molesting you for no reason, or torturing you.

And it had so much food. Most were fat from the excess. She had lost count of how many days she had gone to bed hungry. Her parents tried their best, but life was just so hard. To think she had a place to stay if she ever did escape, gave her renewed hope.

She smiled at her cousin. "I'm glad you're here."

"So am I. I just wish it was under better circumstances."

"I'm sorry about your father. I liked him." She caught herself. "I mean, I like him."

He patted her back. "You know him better than I do. I've barely spoken to him in fifteen years."

"If he were in America, would he survive the cancer?"

"Perhaps. Certainly, he'd have a better chance if it had been caught early enough. But it's too late for him now. At least, though, I got to meet him again, got to know him a little bit, and he got to know me."

"You were lucky to be able to get here. America is our enemy. At least that's what the government says."

"I had a visa granted on compassionate grounds. Unfortunately, though, it's only for a week."

"So short a time."

"Too short."

"I wish you could stay longer. I want to hear about America."

"And I'd love to tell you all about it." He produced another candy bar from his pocket. This one was square and orange. She eagerly snatched it from his fingers.

"What's this one?"

"Reese's Peanut Butter Cup. Almost a tie for my favorite."

"Peanut butter?" She tore the wrapper and took a bite, then froze in place. "This is unbelievable!" she mumbled as she chewed. "This is so good. If I lived in America, I'd eat these every day."

He patted his stomach. "Then expect this to grow a lot."

She giggled. "I'd be willing, if it meant tasting something like this all the time." She swallowed then took another bite, holding up the wrapper. "Why are they so small? These things look bigger on TV."

"They normally are. These are what we call Halloween candy. I brought a couple of boxes worth. They're small so didn't take up a lot of room in my suitcase."

"Halloween candy?"

"Yes."

"What's that?"

"Halloween. October thirty-first. It's where kids get dressed up in costumes and go door to door and people give them candy."

Her eyes shot wide. "They *give* you it?"

"Yep."

"America truly is the most wonderful country in the world!"

He chuckled. "Well, I like to think so, but not because of our candy bars, though that's definitely one of the reasons."

Another giggle escaped as she polished off the peanut butter cup. She smiled up at her cousin as they continued toward the market. He was unlike anyone she had ever met. So handsome, so funny, so worldly. He caught her staring, and she looked away. "Can I ask a question?"

"Of course."

Butterflies fluttered in her stomach. "How do you know when you're in love?"

He regarded her. "*Are* you in love?"

"I...I don't know. I've never been in love before, so how would I know?"

He stopped then faced her. "Is there someone in particular?"

Her cheeks flushed. "No, not really."

"I see. Well, you know how I know when I'm in love?"

"How?" She sounded a little too eager.

"When I can picture myself singing all those love songs to someone. When the words make sense, *that's* when I know I'm in love."

She smiled. It made perfect sense. She had listened to countless love songs her entire life, knew the words to lots of them by heart, though had never felt them. Sure, she had pictured singing some of them to crushes, yet they were just words. But now, everything just made sense— all the words finally made sense.

He smiled. "So, is there someone? Someone you can picture?"

She turned away, resuming their walk toward the market, and lied. "No."

"Well, that's all right. You're still young. There's plenty of time for that." He froze, putting a hand out to stop her. "I want you to go home. Right now."

"What do you mean? Why?"

Diego stared at her firmly. "Just do what I say. Now. Turn around, go home. Don't stop. Just walk away."

She went numb, devastated. What had she said? What had upset him so much that he no longer wanted to be with her?

"Go. Now!" he hissed.

Her eyes filled with tears but she turned, reluctantly walking away, the taste of the sweet treat still in her mouth, ruined by the betrayal. She replayed the conversation, struggling to find something she might have said that had offended him—something she could apologize for to make things better, to make things the way they were.

A shout startled her. She flinched at the sound—loud, angry. She wiped her eyes dry with her knuckles and turned to see her cousin standing with his hands up. Several police officers, weapons drawn, surrounded him. A wave of relief washed over her as she realized he wasn't mad at her—he was protecting her.

But that was quickly pushed aside by fear.

"What's this all about?" he asked.

"On your knees! Hands clasped behind your head!"

He complied, offering no resistance. He could have fought them, she was sure. He was an American soldier. He could beat these men if he was given the chance. Yet he was unarmed and outnumbered, and besides, he had done nothing wrong. His only crime was walking while American.

One of the men rushed forward and handcuffed him before hauling him to his feet.

"May I ask what's going on?"

A man in a suit approached, a cigar clamped between his teeth. "You are an American spy," he growled, "and before I'm through with you, you'll tell me everything I want to know."

"I think you've got me mistaken for someone else."

"No. You are Corporal Diego Mendoza, United States Army. And a spy." The man stepped closer, blowing smoke into her cousin's face. He didn't react. "Your life as you know it is over, traitor."

She tore her eyes away from the scene, forcing herself to walk away.

"Stop that girl!" shouted the man with the cigar.

She bolted. Orders erupted behind her, commanding her to stop, but fear ruled her now. Everything around her became a distant echo. She darted down an alleyway, running as fast as she could. Cutting across another street, she glanced over her shoulder, seeing no one, and darted down another alleyway and out of sight.

She needed to get away, away from the police, from this place. But where could she go? This was Venezuela, and there was no escaping the authorities. Yet she had to tell someone what had just happened.

She spotted a bus, its destination displayed on the front. She waited for it to pass then sprinted after it. A boy she recognized from the streets held out his hand as he sat on the bumper. She took it, and he hauled her beside him as the bus continued along.

"Where are you heading?" asked the boy.

"Caracas."

He rolled his eyes. "No shit. I mean, where in Caracas?"

She thought for a moment, her mind still processing everything that had happened. She could think of only one place to go.

"The American Embassy."

Embassy of the United States of America

Caracas, Venezuela

Ryan Price stretched his left arm in front of him as far as he could. He had done something to his back. What, he wasn't sure. When he had gone to bed, he was fine, but he woke up with a pain between his shoulder blades that he just couldn't get rid of. It felt like something had to pop, as if there was a pocket of gas trapped, demanding release. He gripped his wrist, pulling even harder, the pain increasing.

A rap at his door ended his chiropractic experimentation.

"Come in."

The door opened and Mia Turner poked her head inside. She opened her mouth to say something then stopped, giving him a puzzled look. "You okay, Chief?"

He rotated his shoulder several times, stretching out his neck. "I don't know. I did something to my back. Just feels like it needs a good pop or crack, or I don't know what."

She smirked. "Maybe it's a tumor."

"It's not a tumor!" he snapped in a near-perfect Arnold Schwarzenegger imitation.

She snickered and entered the room. "I could try to massage it out for you."

He grunted. "Great. And in twenty years, you'll accuse me of sexual assault."

She regarded him for a moment. "Actually, wouldn't *you* be accusing *me*?"

He shrugged. "I don't know. I think it's best we keep our hands to ourselves these days, don't you?"

"Probably." She held up her tablet. "Something I think you need to see."

"Oh?"

She handed him the device, a personnel file showing tombstone information for a US Army corporal displayed.

"What am I looking at?"

"About an hour ago, a young girl—thirteen years old—came to the main gate crying. Claimed her American cousin had been arrested."

"By whom?"

"The police."

"Really?" He leaned back, grimacing for a moment as he scrolled through the limited information. "This is him?"

"If she's telling us the truth, yes. He was properly registered with us, had a visa to visit on compassionate grounds. Apparently, his father's dying. He arrived Friday, due to go back this Friday."

"And we're sure this is the guy?"

"Yes. I set up a digital lineup. She picked out his photo right away. There's no doubt about it. This is the guy."

"Do we know anything about him beyond the basics?"

"He's nothing special. He's twenty-eight, currently posted to the Pentagon. He's a nobody. No combat experience. He's just a regular citizen, down here visiting a dying family member, who just happens to be US Army."

Price grunted. As the CIA's Chief of Station Caracas, it was his job to be suspicious, and something didn't smell right. "Have we heard anything from the Venezuelans?"

"Nada."

"Well, they have to have had some reason to arrest him. I would think if it was for propaganda purposes, it'd be all over the news by now." He glanced at the array of screens mounted on the wall to his left, one of them tuned to a local Venezuelan news channel. Nothing. "Okay, here's what we do. Let's treat this like we would any other case, as if it were just a civilian who worked for Walmart. Contact the Ministry of People's Power—what a ridiculous name—and tell them we have reason to believe they arrested one of our citizens and would like an explanation—and an opportunity to talk to him. Contact the Pentagon. Let them know that one of their people has been arrested. And keep my name out of it."

Turner arched an eyebrow. "Sir?"

"Caracas knows who I am. If they think any of the inquiries are coming from this office, they're going to immediately assume they've caught a spy."

She lowered her voice. "Have they?"

He chuckled. "Well, if they did, it's news to me." He handed her back the tablet. "Keep me posted."

"Will do." She left, and he couldn't help but check out her ass. Spectacular. His divorce hadn't gone through yet, but he was single. His ex-wife had been fed up with their postings around the world. Reopening the embassy in Caracas had been the last straw. She couldn't stand the heat, and she had given an ultimatum—"We leave, or I leave." Leaving for him wasn't an option. He would have to give up his career, and he had worked too damn hard to get to where he was.

Chief of Station in Venezuela was an important job. Venezuela was considered an enemy, and the new president had decided reopening the embassy with minimal staff, including a CIA component, was in the country's best interest. If he served here successfully, he could get one of the bigger jobs—Moscow or Beijing were the dream assignments.

He had loved his wife, but they had drifted apart over the years. What had once been a curse had turned into a blessing. Her inability to have children made their separation far less messy. His life was a hell of a lot simpler now. More peaceful.

Though he was as horny as hell.

And Turner was exactly his type.

Sexy with a pulse.

He grimaced, his back protesting again.

I should have taken her up on her offer.

The Oval Office, The White House
Washington, DC

"Anything else?"

Charlotte Collins, the National Security Advisor, stepped forward. "One last thing that's not in the Brief. It came in as I was on my way here."

President Christopher Hayes suppressed his frown. When elected, he hadn't realized just how many meetings would occupy his day. From the moment he left the official residence in the morning until he returned—at God only knew what hour—every single moment, every single minute, was scheduled. Even his free time was scheduled—fifteen minutes each day for lunch with his family.

If there wasn't some crisis.

And there was always something.

"What is it?"

"It looks like an American citizen has been arrested in Venezuela."

He leaned back in his chair, folding his arms. "Venezuela? Not exactly a vacation hotspot. Do we care?"

"Yes, sir. Turns out he's US Army."

Hayes groaned. "US Army? What the hell is he doing in Venezuela? Please tell me we didn't send him."

"No, sir. He's on personal leave. He was born there. Left the country over fifteen years ago. His father is dying of cancer so the Venezuelan Embassy granted him a visa on compassionate grounds."

"How nice of them. Was that before or after they decided they were going to arrest him?"

"No idea."

"If they interrogate him, does he know anything?"

"No, sir. He's just a corporal. He works at the loading dock at the Pentagon. Minimal security clearance. According to the information I have on him, his job is to make sure the cafeterias have whatever they need to keep feeding the brass."

"So, he's a stock boy?"

"For lack of a better term, I suppose he is."

"Well, if he's stupid enough to voluntarily go to a country that's our sworn enemy, then he deserves whatever he gets. I don't want to waste political capital on a moron. Let the embassy down there handle it. Register the usual protest, blah blah blah. I don't want to waste any time on fools."

A throat cleared at the back of the room and a man who rarely spoke stepped forward.

"You've got something to add, Leif?"

Leif Morrison, Deputy Director of CIA for Operations, frowned. "I'm afraid so, Mr. President. But I'll need the room."

Leroux/White Residence, Fairfax Towers

Falls Church, Virginia

"May I join you?"

CIA Analyst Supervisor Chris Leroux grinned at his girlfriend, CIA Operations Officer Sherrie White, as she poked her head into the shower. "Have I ever said 'no'?"

She stepped inside and closed the frosted glass door, buck naked. He stepped aside to let the slightly shorter spy get under the water as he admired her body. She was gorgeous, and for the longest time, he had believed he didn't deserve her. Part of him still felt that way, though he was coming around. The fact she was still with him was pretty good evidence that she was happy. If she wasn't, she could leave him and find another man in a heartbeat.

The old adage that opposites attract was certainly proven true in their case.

"Want to soap me up?"

He gave a toothy grin to the back of her head. "Um, is the Pope Catholic?"

She twisted her head and smirked. "I thought he was Triarii."

Leroux snorted. "You read that file?"

"Oh yeah. Acton and Palmer's files are two of the most interesting I've ever read. The professors do get around."

"You're right about that." Leroux began soaping up his girlfriend's back. She arched, her backside pressing against him, Junior immediately taking notice. He reached around, continuing to lather her up. "I'm gonna miss you."

"I should hope so."

He wrapped his arms around her and held her tight. "Be careful."

"It's only Lithuania. Nothing to worry about."

"Anything involving the Russians is something to worry about."

"I doubt they'd do anything too crazy."

"Listen, I read the briefing notes. If they are pre-positioning assets to disrupt communications and power, that has to mean they're getting ready for an invasion. If you're able to prove that—if you interfere with those plans—they won't hesitate to kill you."

"Then I guess I'm just going to have to kill them first."

"At least you'll have Jack with you."

"Yep. He's always good on a mission. Hot as hell too."

A flash of jealousy tore through him, and he backed off. She reached around and grabbed his favorite body part.

"You know I was just joking. You're the only man for me." She turned her head again, eying him. "You know that, right?"

He looked away. "Yeah, yeah. I guess I just don't have a good sense of humor when it comes to that stuff."

"You're right, I'm sorry." She delivered a Cheshire grin. "I think I should be punished."

He smiled. "I think so."

She drew closer, Junior at full mast when his phone rang on the counter, the coded ring indicating it was his second-in-command, Senior Analyst Sonya Tong. Sherrie cursed. "It's like that woman knows the second your penis goes active."

He snorted, shoving the showerhead to spray against the wall before opening the shower door. He reached out and grabbed the phone. He swiped his thumb, taking the call, placing it on speaker before setting it back down on the vanity.

"Hi, Sonya. Kinda busy right now."

Sherrie rubbed up against him, and he gave her a look. She merely continued with a naughty smile.

"The Chief's called us in. Priority mission."

He arched an eyebrow as Sherrie reached down and took control. "What's up?"

"A US Army corporal has been arrested by the Venezuelans for espionage. The Chief wants us to find out where he's being held."

Sherrie leaned back, and they both groaned.

"Did I call at a bad time?"

Forgetting where he was for a moment, he replied, "Um, no. Just taking a shower. Recall the team. Get an ops center assigned. I'll be there in twenty."

Sherrie held up three fingers.

"Make that thirty."

"Okay, boss. I'm on it. Enjoy your shower."

"I will."

He ended the call, and Sherrie pressed her hands against the shower wall, pushing back on him. "You're damn right he's going to enjoy it."

He snickered then closed his eyes.

I'm the luckiest damn man in the world.

1st Special Forces Operational Detachment—Delta HQ

Fort Liberty, North Carolina

A.k.a. "The Unit"

"So, how is it?"

Atlas groaned in pleasure as he chewed. He held up a hand to cover his mouth, unable to wait to deliver his verdict. "Holy shit, babe, this is unbelievable!"

His girlfriend, Vanessa Moore, beamed at him. "Are you sure you're not just saying that?"

He dismissed the suggestion with a swipe of a meaty paw. "Of course not. Would I lie to you?"

Atlas' best friend, Niner, snickered. "If you know what's good for you."

Atlas eyeballed the much smaller Korean American. "You're telling me that this isn't some of the most amazing food truck fare you've eaten?"

Niner took another bite of his wrap, holding up a finger as he chewed then swallowed. "I didn't say that at all."

"Good."

"But let's be honest. If it tasted like kangaroo shit, you'd still be raving."

Atlas shrugged. "That's because I love my woman." He took another bite. "Fortunately for me"—he chewed—"everything she cooks is incredible."

Dawson, leaning against the side of the truck, chuckled. "And sometimes dangerous."

Vanessa leaned out the window. "Dangerous? Oh, you mean that time he"—she jabbed a finger at Atlas—"had Niner eating that ghost pepper?"

Niner groaned, taking an involuntary step back. "Oh my God, I forgot about that. You almost killed me!"

"You asked for it," said Atlas.

Vanessa lowered her voice. "You two keep it down. I don't want customers thinking my food kills people."

Niner deadpanned, "Food doesn't kill people. People kill people."

Atlas polished off his wrap. "If we die, we die."

Sergeant Will "Spock" Lightman agreed as he toasted the group with his half-eaten sandwich. "But what a way to go, eh?"

A horn honked and everyone turned to see Maggie Dawson pulling up with a load of other halves. Doors swung open, and a bevy of beauties stepped out, eagerly rushing toward the food truck set up behind the

Unit. The group had received permission for the cold opening after their commanding officer, Colonel Thomas Clancy, put in a good word.

Vanessa had been training for years to become a chef, had finally graduated, and after serving in the trenches, had decided she wanted to be her own boss. A restaurant of her own wasn't in the budget, but a food truck was. Atlas had wholeheartedly agreed, supporting her all the way. It was the beginning of her dream, and he would do everything possible to make it come true.

Maggie rushed up and gave her husband a kiss.

"What took you so long?" asked Dawson.

"Well, you're not going to believe what happened. Some guy showed up with a car on the back of a tow truck asking to donate it for target practice on the range."

"Donate it?" Atlas' eyes narrowed. "I don't think I've ever heard of that before."

Dawson shrugged. "I can't say that I have either, but I guess they have to come from somewhere."

Angela Hanwood, Niner's girlfriend, nodded vigorously. "Yeah, he said, 'If they've given up on me, then I'm giving up on them.'"

Spock cocked an eyebrow. "What kind of car was it?"

"Something sporty. British, I think."

"British and sporty?" Atlas snorted. "Let me guess, with a leaping jungle cat on the hood?"

"That would be the one."

Atlas smirked. "Well, that would explain it. Have you seen their new commercial?"

Niner's head bobbed as he finished off Vanessa's creation. "If you're talking about that ridiculous thing that looks like they're advertising fashion from a 1960s Star Trek episode worn by androgynous actors who've lost the ability to smile, then yeah, I've seen it."

Maggie turned to her husband. "Wait a minute. Is that the video you showed me last week?"

"Yep."

"I had no idea that was for a car company. I thought it was a fashion line by a company run by a teenager whose daddy decided to humor her."

"Nope. They've abandoned everything they've ever done, changed their logo, everything, and decided to target zero-point-zero-one percent of the market."

"Well, somebody's going to be losing their job."

"If whoever is responsible doesn't, they're all going to be losing their jobs."

"How are things going here?"

Everyone turned to see Colonel Clancy strolling toward them. They all belonged to 1st Special Forces Operational Detachment—Delta, commonly known to the American public as the Delta Force, in no small part due to the awesome Chuck Norris movie that created a Unit tradition—everyone, even though most weren't born when the movies came out, loved eighties action flicks starring staples like Stallone, Schwarzenegger, and Norris.

Vanessa waved at the colonel. "Hello, sir! Things are going great so far."

"Good to hear," Clancy said, standing in front of the truck and staring up at the menu. "What's good?"

Atlas replied in his impossibly deep voice. "Everything, sir."

Clancy snickered, jerking a thumb at him. "You've got the sergeant well-trained."

Vanessa winked at Atlas. "He's definitely scoring points today."

Atlas held out a palm surreptitiously behind his back, and Niner gave him a low-five.

"I'll tell you what, surprise me. I'm sure everything is good, but I'll trust the chef's choice." He turned toward Dawson. "I've got some bad news for you guys."

Dawson's eyebrows climbed. "Oh?"

"I'm going to have to break up this little party. You're being deployed."

Maggie gripped Dawson's arm, staring up at him, not bothering to ask the obvious question—as Clancy's assistant, she would know soon enough.

But that didn't stop Angela. "Can you tell us where?"

"Sorry, classified. You guys finish up. Briefing in ten minutes." Clancy smiled at Vanessa. "Have one of the guys bring it in for me."

"Of course, Colonel."

Clancy headed back toward the Unit, wagging a finger at Niner. "Just make sure it's not him. I don't trust that he won't take a bite out of it before it reaches me."

Everyone roared with laughter, and Niner held up his hands. "Hey, that happened one time!"

Atlas eyeballed his friend. "Yeah, but dude, it was the *colonel's* sandwich."

"How was I supposed to know? I had half a dozen sandwiches and I was hungry. I just took a bite of one, not all of them."

"You're not supposed to take a bite of any of them."

Vanessa leaned out, holding a container. "Atlas, you bring the colonel's order to him."

"Sure thing, babe." Atlas grabbed the box, giving her a peck on the cheek. "Good luck today, babe, but I'm sure you don't need it."

She smiled. "Thanks." Then her eyes widened. "Uh oh."

Atlas stared at her, concerned. "What?"

She jerked her chin behind him toward the Unit. At least a dozen people were emerging for their lunch, explaining why the colonel had come when he had.

"You got this, babe. I'll try to come out and see how you're doing when I get a chance."

But she was already past the goodbyes. "Maggie, can you give me a hand?"

Maggie bounced on her toes, excited. "Absolutely! I've never worked in a food truck before. Is it anything like the movie Chef?" she asked as she rushed toward the door.

Niner snickered. "I'm sure it's exactly like that. Just remember, if it gets hot in there, put cornstarch on your balls."

Atlas' fist shot out, punching Niner on the shoulder, the impact shoving him several feet.

Niner winced, rubbing it gingerly. "I deserved that." He turned to Dawson. "Are you going to hit me too?"

Dawson replied. "Yeah, but I'm not going to let you know when. It could be today. It could be tomorrow. Hell, it could be two years from now. But one of these days, I'm going to drop you for suggesting my wife has balls."

"Lady balls," Niner corrected.

Dawson jerked his chin toward the Unit. "Let's go, gentlemen and Niner. We've got a briefing to attend."

Unknown Location

Venezuela

"I'm an American citizen! I know my rights! I am entitled to talk to someone from my embassy!"

The words were gasped out, one at a time, and it meant the waterboarding was yet again ineffective. Colonel Luis Herrera stood in the corner, in the shadows, his arms folded, his back against the wall, his feet crossed at the ankles. The prisoner's resilience was impressive. It had been over 24 hours of constant interrogation—ear-piercing sounds, intensely bright lights, sleep deprivation, waterboarding. None of it had broken the man. He simply continually repeated his demand to see someone from the American embassy.

Herrera smirked. "You have no rights here." His voice echoed from the darkness as he remained out of sight.

Mendoza's head spun toward the sound, his eyes squinting. "Who are you?"

"I'm the person who decides whether you live or die."

"Bullshit! I'm an American citizen. There is no way in hell someone like you has the authority to kill me."

Herrera chuckled. The man was right. But also wrong. The authority had already been granted to him. It was his decision. This American wouldn't be the first person he had ordered executed, and certainly wouldn't be the last. Venezuela had its enemies, foreign and domestic, and it was his job to identify and deal with threats, specifically those from outside their borders.

He leaned forward. "You're right, Corporal Mendoza. I don't have the authority to order your death, but those who do have granted me that power in this situation. If I decide you should be executed, you will be."

"Why? What the hell do you think I've done?"

"You don't know?"

"Of course, I don't know, because I've done nothing wrong! I just came here to visit my father before he died. You know this! It was all in the visa application, which your government approved!"

Herrera chuckled again. "You realize how many people lie on their visa applications? Especially you Americans. An American soldier comes to Venezuela with nothing but good intentions, to see his dying father one last time, to visit the family he left behind when he fled the country after that same father was arrested. Foolish."

"I'm not here for anything political. My father was never a political activist. He's an old man. He's dying. That's all."

Herrera leaned forward, sneering. "Obviously, you're here to continue your father's work and provide the American government with assistance in furthering its goal of overthrowing the duly elected government of Venezuela, chosen by the people."

Mendoza snorted. "Chosen by the people? Give me a break. Your elections are as fair as Russia's."

Herrera's eyes narrowed. "So, you have political views about your former homeland?"

"No. I mean, I believe every country should be a democracy, but that's up to its people. I'm just here to see my father. He never was a political activist, and even if he was, he certainly isn't anymore. You took everything from him. He's not the threat."

"I agree. You are. America is."

Mendoza glared. "I'm not here as a representative of my government. I'm here as a son coming to visit his father before he passes. I have no opinion on my government's position. In fact, I don't even know what my government's position is."

"I find that hard to believe."

"You seem to know a great deal about me. I'm a corporal. Do you think we give a shit about politics? International politics? I make sure the brass at the Pentagon gets fed. That's all. I know what kind of noodles the general likes, what kind of taco shells the admiral likes, and when they're in town, I make sure it's in stock. That's it."

Herrera smirked. "So, you know the comings and goings of your military leaders."

Mendoza released an exasperated sigh. "You're wasting your time with me. I know nothing of importance. I visited my father, said my goodbyes, and made my peace with him. Just let me go, put me on a plane, and send me back to the States. Nobody has to know about this."

"Unfortunately, people already know, thanks to another traitor in your family."

Mendoza appeared taken aback. "I'm sure I don't know what you're talking about."

"Your cousin," Herrera said, his tone sharp. "She was spotted entering the American embassy yesterday after we arrested you."

Mendoza's face twisted in concern. "Is she all right?"

Herrera suppressed a smirk. He had found his leverage, the concern in the man's voice and on his face unmistakable. He cared for his cousin. "She is. For now. But should I decide she's a threat, she won't be."

"She's thirteen years old! How the hell is she a threat?"

Herrera raised an eyebrow. "She may not be a threat today, but in time, she very well could be. How do you think she'd feel if I killed you? Would she hate her government? Would she seek to overthrow it? Would she join the rebels? If I eliminate her now, it's one less problem we have to deal with in ten years."

Mendoza's voice broke. "But she's just a kid."

"Today, yes. But tomorrow, she could be a leader of a rebellion. Perhaps I *should* have her eliminated."

"No! You can't do that!"

Herrera leaned closer. "Well, if she's so important to you, then you decide. Tell me what I want to know, and she lives. Don't, and she doesn't. A simple black-and-white choice. Make it now."

Mendoza's shoulders slumped in defeat. "What do you want to know?"

"I want to know why you're here. And don't tell me it's to see your dying father. I don't believe a word you wrote on that visa application."

"What do you want me to say? I'll sign anything. Just don't hurt her. Don't hurt my family."

"I don't want some false confession. I want the truth."

"But you don't want to hear the truth."

"I do."

"I've already told you the truth."

Herrera stepped out of the shadows, holding up a photo—a surveillance photo. "If you're here to visit your father, then explain this."

Operations Center 3, CIA Headquarters

Langley, Virginia

Chris Leroux was all smiles as he entered the state-of-the-art operations center, most of his team already assembled, including the ever-punctual Sonya Tong, who beamed a smile at him. He returned it as his team greeted him.

"Any luck finding our guy?" he asked as he set himself up at his station in the center of the room.

Tong swiveled her chair to face him. "Sort of. We know where he was arrested, though that's thanks to his thirteen-year-old cousin."

Leroux cocked an eyebrow. "Really?"

"Yeah. Everything we know is based on what she told embassy staff in Caracas. We got lucky. We've got quite a few birds that overpass that area, just because of the situation there. We happened to catch a few minutes of footage, which allowed us to track where he was initially taken. It was just a local police station."

"There's no way they're holding him there."

"Agreed."

"What are we doing to find him?"

Randy Child, the team's wunderkind, spun in his chair, staring at the ceiling. "I'm trying to pull every piece of video footage I can from the area, see if we can catch anything on it." He jerked a thumb at the next station. "Packman is going through comms traffic, seeing if we can find any reference to the arrest."

Packman reported. "Nothing specific so far, but there was a burst of chatter from that area around the time of the arrest."

"Anything over the air?" asked Leroux.

"Nothing that wasn't encrypted. We're working on cracking it, but I'm not very optimistic. We already know from reports that the Chinese have provided them with some pretty advanced comms gear. So have the Russians."

"Lovely," Leroux muttered. "Can we at least figure out where the calls were coming from and going to?"

"Some of it, yeah. It looks like there's a good amount of chatter between that town and SEBIN headquarters."

"And is that normal?"

Tong folded her arms as she leaned back. "Nope. I did an analysis of intercepts over the past thirty days. There's been more chatter between that town and the secret police in the past day than during the rest of the month combined. From what we can tell, it's a small community. Unimportant. Nothing going on there. One of the more peaceful areas. Locals are mostly farmers who just want to grow their crops and keep out of trouble. These are peaceful people."

Leroux pinched his chin. "A peaceful town with peaceful people. This type of arrest was probably the most exciting thing they've seen in a long time. Anything on social media? Did somebody record something?"

Tong poured cold water on the idea. "Negative. Nothing we've been able to find yet. Like I said, poor, simple people. And even if they did record it, I doubt they'd post it. They'd be too scared to."

"You're right. These people are looking to avoid trouble, and one way to ensure trouble is to show you witnessed someone neck-deep in it." Leroux smacked his hands together. "All right, let's work the problem. We know he was taken to the police station. Once he was transferred into secret police custody, the comms traffic likely would have died off. They don't give a shit about keeping the locals informed. That's our window. Figure out every place they could have taken him—every known headquarters, regional headquarters, black sites, anything. Figure out the travel time from the police station to those locations. That's our surveillance window."

Packman gave a thumbs-up.

"And check our footage. We've got eyes on most places. Let's put them to use. We need to find our man so Delta can go in and get him."

"We're on it, boss," Tong replied, and Leroux smiled at her, staring a little longer than he should. He was in a committed relationship, but he was fully aware Tong loved him and had for some time. And he was also fully aware that he had feelings for her too. If Sherrie weren't in the picture, could the two of them end up together?

She caught him staring, and he quickly turned his head away, his cheeks burning. He had to shake these feelings. Every time he gave in to them, even just slightly, he was racked with guilt. Sherrie was an amazing woman who loved him for who he was, had given him his confidence, and made him incredibly happy.

He loved her with all his heart.

Yet he couldn't help but wonder what it meant if he also loved someone else. He never intended to act upon it, but he sometimes fantasized about it. Was that cheating? Or just being human? He sighed and caught Tong stealing a glance at him from the corner of her eye.

It certainly felt like cheating.

Embassy of the United States of America

Caracas, Venezuela

Valeria shoveled the food into her face. She was starving, and there seemed to be a never-ending supply of it here. She was on her third generous helping of what the woman had called mac and cheese, the most delicious thing she had ever tasted. It was remarkable, and she couldn't get enough. She couldn't recall the last time she had eaten so much. In fact, there was a good chance she never had before. She reached down and pressed her hand against her stomach—it was protruding slightly. She smiled.

So, this is what it's like to be fat.

She didn't care. She kept eating, struggling to remember to chew and enjoy the flavor sensation. She was accustomed to eating fast. If one of her brothers finished before her, too often, they stole food off her plate. Her mother would scold them, but by then it was too late—the food was gone. Sometimes, her father would give her some of his meal, but she didn't like to accept it. He was a man and was hungry too. Everyone deserved to eat. No one should ever go hungry. Man, woman, or child.

She swallowed then sucked on her straw, delicious Coca-Cola washing over her tongue, ice-cold. She had lost track of how many she had enjoyed since she arrived at the American Embassy. Another unending supply.

The door to the room opened, and she leaped to her feet as the woman named Mia Turner entered with a smile and gestured toward the almost-empty plate.

"Do you want more?"

Valeria nodded vigorously then slumped her shoulders as she held her stomach. "I do, but I shouldn't. I think I'm going to be sick if I eat any more."

Turner chuckled and motioned for her to sit. She did, pushing the plate away and focusing instead on her drink, gripping it in both hands, her elbows resting on the arms of her chair, the straw stuck in her mouth.

"Careful. Drink too many of those, and you won't sleep for days if you're not used to it."

Valeria stared at the woman, her eyes wide. "Really?"

"Caffeine. It's like drinking coffee. Have you ever had coffee?"

"Sure. It's horrible."

"It's an acquired taste."

"Have you heard anything about my cousin?"

"Not yet. We're making inquiries."

Valeria placed her can of Coke on the table, the sugar delivery vessel disappointingly empty. Turner pushed a bottle of water across the table.

"Drink this instead. And if you feel the urge, burp. You're not used to drinking carbonated beverages—they're loaded with gas."

Valeria hesitated as she cracked the cap on the bottle. "Gas? Like in your car?"

"A different type. Carbon dioxide. It causes the bubbles. When you drink, the bubbles go into your stomach. You're going to either burp them out or fart them out."

Valeria snickered then shoved her shoulders back and belched. She giggled, and Turner tossed her head back, laughing hard.

"Oh, girl, that's one for the books." Turner became serious. "Is there anything else you can tell me? Anything at all? Even the smallest detail might help."

Valeria shrugged, having racked her brain all day, desperate to remember some detail she had forgotten that might help. "I think I told you everything. I'm sorry."

"And you have no idea why the police arrested him?"

"No. He did nothing wrong. We were just going to the market. We were walking then he told me to go home. He knew before I did that something bad was happening."

"Did you recognize the police that arrested him?"

"Some of them, I think. I don't know. When you see the police, you usually head in the opposite direction, and you never make eye contact."

"Even in a small town like yours?"

"Some of them are local, sure. Locals you've grown up with. But too many of them are from out of town. They like to do that."

"Why?"

"My uncle says it's because of favoritism. If your police are strangers, they don't let you get away with as much."

"Your uncle sounds like a wise man."

"He is." Her shoulders slumped. "He was. He's not the same since he got sick."

"No, I suppose not. Do you know who your uncle is?"

"What do you mean?"

"Do you know that he was arrested years ago for being a revolutionary?"

"My mom said that was nonsense. She said he was accused by a neighbor because my uncle refused to split the cost of a new fence the neighbor knocked down while drunk. He said it was his responsibility to pay for it himself. I guess the neighbor got mad and told the police that my uncle was anti-Chávez. He's just a farmer. Nothing more. There aren't revolutionaries in our town. Everybody's given up. They just want to be left alone."

"You sound sure of this."

"I can only tell you what my mother said. I'm thirteen. I don't really know much about these things."

"Really? When I was thirteen, I remember a lot of conversations taking place around me because people thought I wasn't paying attention, but I always listened."

Valeria turned away, embarrassed. "Yeah, I suppose that's true. Adults don't really notice you. They think you're always just looking at your phone or have your headphones on."

"So, you have heard things?"

"Sure, but nothing about rebels or revolutions. Just what neighbors are sleeping with other neighbors." She snickered. "It's like a soap opera. Who needs TV?" She sighed, melancholy sweeping over her. "Our TV is broken, and we can't afford to fix it. I have to go to a friend's house if I want to see anything."

"You can get most things over the Internet now."

"Yeah, but you have to be choosy with your data. Everything is so expensive, according to my mother."

"How can you afford it?"

"We can't. My uncle pays for it."

"I thought he was a poor farmer."

Valeria flicked her wrist. "I don't know. All I know is I want to go to America. Life is so much better there."

"What makes you think that?"

"I've seen it on TV, in movies. I've read about it in books and magazines. I've seen it on the Internet. Big houses, lots of food. No one's ever hungry, no one's ever thirsty. No one's ever cold or hot. You always have a roof over your head, food in your stomach. Big schools, libraries, concerts." A wistful sigh escaped. "I would have died to see Taylor Swift."

"Maybe one day you will."

She groaned. "Not if I'm stuck here." She jerked forward, her elbows on the table, leaning closer to the woman. "Could you get me to America?"

"What about your family?"

"Well, if you could get all of us, that would be even better."

The corner of the woman's mouth curled up. "That's not exactly what I meant."

Valeria leaned back. "I see. Well, as long as I knew they'd be happy, I could go alone. Diego said I could stay with him if I ever made it to America."

"He said that?"

She nodded.

"That's nice of him. You two must have gotten very close."

Her cheeks flushed, a tingle sweeping through her. "I suppose."

The woman smiled slightly. "He's handsome, isn't he?"

Valeria looked down, her hands fidgeting. "I suppose so."

Turner leaned closer. "Listen, we're going to try to find your cousin and get him back. The question I have for you is, do you want to wait here while we do that, or do you want to go home?"

Valeria opened her mouth to reply then stopped. She met the woman's gaze. "*Can* I go home?"

"You can do whatever you want, sweetie. This may not be a free country, but inside these walls we believe in people's right to choose. However, there's little doubt you were seen coming in here. They've probably put two and two together as to who you are and why you're here. It could be dangerous for you to leave."

The color drained from her cheeks. "What about my family? Could they be in danger?"

"It's a definite possibility."

Tears welled in her eyes. "I put them in danger!"

"If they're accusing your cousin of being a spy, they were already in danger."

"I should go to them."

"You could, but we can't protect you once you leave."

"But my family!"

"There's nothing you could do to help them right now."

Valeria bolted to her feet, kicking her chair out behind her. "I have to go to them! I have to warn them! I have to make sure they're all right!"

Turner remained seated. "I think that's a mistake."

"I don't care! You save my cousin, I'll save my family!" She headed for the door, only to find it locked from the outside. "Am I a prisoner here?"

Turner turned in her chair to face her. "Of course not. But I highly recommend you don't leave through the front gate."

"Why?"

"You'll probably be arrested the moment you're on Venezuelan soil."

Her shoulders tensed. "So, what am I going to do?"

Turner rose. "We're going to go for a little walk."

The Unit

Fort Liberty, North Carolina

Dawson stood in front of the displays occupying the front of the operations center at the Unit. This wasn't his normal vantage point. Usually, he was at the other end of a body cam or a comms unit, talking to whoever was Control Actual for the mission he was on. But today, they were going over satellite footage provided by Langley.

"Looks like this was well planned," said Clancy, standing beside him.

Master Sergeant Mike "Red" Belme, second-in-command and Dawson's best friend, agreed. "We have some footage of the arrest, and we can confirm he was taken to this police station, but not much else."

Clancy gestured toward one of the feeds replaying on a loop showing a canopy extending out from the front of the police station. "They go under that thing, then leave. They knew they were being watched, or at least that they could be, so they made sure we couldn't see what the hell was going on."

Dawson ran his fingers through his hair. Twelve vehicles cycled through, then split off in pairs in six different directions. "He could be in any one of them."

Red cursed, his arms folded as the last of the SUVs, all black with heavily tinted windows, pulled back into sight. "And for the ones we've been able to track, at the other end, we can't see them unloading. We've got footage of them arriving at various sites within half a day's drive, but they made sure we couldn't see who got out."

Dawson chewed his cheek as he reviewed the footage for the umpteenth time. There was nothing to be gleaned. The vehicle would pull up under the canopy with all its windows closed, tinted so they couldn't even see the driver, then any number of people would get in or out, unseen.

He squinted, noticing something. He turned back to the controller. "Do we have another angle on this? Something that will show the passenger windows better?"

She held up a finger, whispering into her headset. Moments later, she gave a thumbs-up, jerking her chin at the screen. They all turned as the footage changed to another satellite, this one lower on the horizon, offering a different perspective.

"Zoom in so we've got a better view as they pull away."

Someone executed the request, and the image expanded. Dawson stepped closer, waiting for what he had spotted, then smiled, jabbing his finger. "There it is. Freeze it." The image froze, and he stepped even closer, pointing at what he had spotted. "This is the one."

Clancy squinted at the image. "What am I missing, Sergeant Major?"

"Bring up the footage of the arrest." The footage began playing on another display. Dawson stepped over to it. "These are all local police. Except him." He indicated a man in a business suit, his mouth chomping down on a cigar.

Red scratched at the beginnings of a ginger beard. "He's got a death grip on that thing."

"Exactly, and it's lit in every minute of footage we have of him." Dawson pointed back at the other image. "In that *one* vehicle, the window is slightly down. I'm willing to bet our cigar smoker is in there. He put the window down as a courtesy." He tapped the display. "Follow the cigar, and we'll find our man."

Clancy turned to the controller. "Get that theory to Langley. And make sure you don't say where it came from."

The woman cocked an eyebrow. "Sir?"

"I don't want them recruiting my sergeant major out from under me."

Dawson snorted. "No risk of that, sir. I bleed Army green."

Operations Center 3, CIA Headquarters

Langley, Virginia

"Got them!"

Leroux looked up from his station and turned in his chair to see a triumphant Tong jerking her chin toward the main display. He rose as footage showed two SUVs pulling up to a walled compound then through the gates. "Are you sure it's them?"

Tong gave him the eye, and he chuckled. "Okay, okay, you're sure."

She zoomed in on the lead vehicle. The passenger-side window was still down a crack as it passed through a large set of garage doors that automatically closed as the mini-convoy disappeared inside. "Just in case you had doubts."

He smiled. "Excellent work. I thought you lost him?"

"We did. The jungle canopy was just too damn thick. Some good estimates and hard teamwork, et voilà."

Leroux rose, clasping his hands behind his back. "Good work, everyone. Now we need to figure out if our hunch is right."

"And if it isn't?"

He smirked. "Then we blame Delta. It was their idea."

Danny Packman grinned. "And if we're right?"

"Delta who?"

The entire team broke out in laughter as Leroux approached the screen. "Where is this?"

"San Miguel. About an hour south of Caracas," Tong replied.

"South? I thought the arrest was west of the capital."

"It was. That's what threw us. We assumed, since they were heading east, they'd go to Caracas or one of the other black sites in between. But it turns out they completely avoided the capital and went here instead."

Leroux scratched his chin. "Now, why would they do that?"

"They didn't want to risk him being seen? Too many eyes in Caracas?"

Leroux returned to his chair. "Oh, I can definitely see them avoiding Caracas. Makes perfect sense. Anything could go wrong—car accident, mechanical failure, anything." He gestured toward a map on the right of the main display showing all the known black sites and regional headquarters of the Venezuelan secret police, the *Servicio Bolivariano de Inteligencia Nacional* (SEBIN), or Bolivarian National Intelligence Service. "We had high confidence going into this that they'd take him to one of the black sites outside of the city, but every mile they travel just adds to the risk. Why would they go over a hundred miles beyond where they needed to? Is there anything special about this site?"

Tong stared at her screen, her head slowly shaking. "Nothing. Nothing that stands out, anyway." She tapped a few keys. "I've sent it to your station. Maybe that famous gut of yours will spot something."

Leroux grunted. "Maybe. Let's start going over any footage we have of this location for the past two weeks. See if we can figure out what's so special about it." He fit his headset into place. "Time to let Delta know they've got a destination."

Dawson Residence, Lake in the Pines Apartments

Fayetteville, North Carolina

"How long do you think you'll be gone?" Maggie asked as she helped Dawson pack.

"Hopefully not long enough for you to miss me."

She paused, giving him the eye. "The moment you walk out that door, Mister, I miss you."

He stepped around the bed, extending his arms. She stepped into them, and he held her tight. "And I miss you."

"You be careful."

"I always am."

"Bullshit. Remember, I type up the colonel's comments on your after-action reports."

"You read my after-action reports?"

"No, but the colonel's old school. He handwrites his comments, and I type them up."

"Good thing you've got that security clearance."

"Nothing like yours, I'm sure."

He chuckled. "Common misconception. Top Secret is Top Secret. It's the need-to-know aspect that keeps things compartmentalized." He wagged a finger with a smirk. "Just don't be sharing anything you read with friends."

She gave him the stink eye. "You know I know better than that."

He gave her a peck on the forehead. "I know. That's why the colonel trusts you. Otherwise, he'd be two-finger typing that stuff himself."

"Like the brass probably wants him to. Yeah, he's definitely a hunt-and-peck kind of guy."

"The best course I ever took in high school was typing."

She regarded him, surprised. "*You* took typing in high school?"

"Yep."

"Why?"

"To meet chicks."

She swatted him as she returned to the dresser. "You're terrible."

"Yes, yes, I am." He returned to packing. "So, how did the rest of the opening go?"

"Fantastic. The comment cards were wonderful, and she sold out of everything."

"Sold?"

Maggie paused. "I don't know. Ran out, I guess, is a better way of putting it when you're not charging." She tossed him his backup charger, and he stuffed it into the bag.

"I just hope the real opening goes as well. People are kind when they're being given free food."

Maggie paused. "Yeah, I was thinking the same thing." She frowned. "I really hope this goes well for her," she said, then lowered her voice as if someone might be eavesdropping. "Do you know that Atlas paid for the whole thing?"

"He didn't mention it, but I suspected it. Vanessa was a student and didn't come from much. Not much opportunity to save."

"From what she was saying, I think he drained all his savings. If this doesn't work, they lose everything."

Dawson pursed his lips as he zipped up the bag. "Then let's hope it works out." He lifted the bag by the straps and gave it a jerk, redistributing the weight inside. "I guess we'll have to make sure anytime we're craving fast food, we stop by the truck instead of going through a drive-through."

"Let's hope we're not her only two customers."

Dawson headed from the bedroom with the bag, Maggie following. "Oh, don't worry about that. Everybody at the Unit will be going just to support Atlas. He's well-liked. She's lucky she's dating him and not Niner."

Maggie giggled. "Oh, everybody likes Niner."

Dawson turned and winked at her, dropping the bag by the door. He shoved his feet into his boots and Maggie dropped to one knee to tie them. He stared down at her, spotting the slight deviation in her hair from a scar she had received when she had been shot. It was barely noticeable, so much so that perhaps he was just imagining it. It felt like so long ago, yet it wasn't.

She gave a final tug on his laces then stood. He wrapped his arms around her, and she hugged him tightly, a long, deep embrace. He stared into her eyes, smiling, then gave her a kiss. Nothing sexual. This was a goodbye. And every time he delivered it, there was a chance this could be their last one. He always wanted it to be something she could remember—something romantic, nothing tawdry. He attempted to repeat, as best he could, the way they had first kissed at their wedding, a memory he would cherish for the rest of his life.

Their lips parted, and her eyes glistened slightly. She was scared—she always was, though she was getting better at hiding it.

"Gotta go, babe."

"I'll see you when I see you."

He grinned, giving her another peck on the top of her head. "I'll see you when I see you, babe."

He picked up his bag and opened the door, stepping out into the hallway and closing it behind him. There was a slight thud, as there always was. He wasn't sure what caused it, though he had a theory. He had stood there once, gathering himself, and caught her gentle sobs on the other side of the door.

It had broken his heart.

He swiftly headed for the stairwell. He didn't want to hear it again. This life was hard. Hard on everyone. Not just the soldiers who had volunteered to serve, but their families who sacrificed every day. The spouses that stayed behind, knowing their loved ones were in harm's way, were heroes as well. They held down the home front while their partners went off to defend the way of life they cherished. They ensured their partner wouldn't have to worry about things falling apart while they were away.

His wife was back home, taking care of everything so he could have a home to return to, a place to decompress, relax, and try to put behind him whatever he had seen, done, or experienced in the name of God and country. He had never appreciated what married life meant until he and Maggie had gotten together. She took care of things, doing so much for him, making his life easier.

But most importantly, she had given him yet another reason to fight. To live. To survive.

To return home.

To return to a home he could have never imagined, to a woman who loved him more than he had ever known, a woman brave enough to fall in love with him, despite knowing what he did, and how distinct the possibility was that he might never return.

It was why he always gave her a proper goodbye.

As he headed down the stairs, he compartmentalized his feelings, shutting them off for the mission ahead. Thoughts of home were a distraction, and distractions could get you killed.

And there was no damn way he was dying.

Not when he had finally found the woman of his dreams.

Caracas, Venezuela

It was everything Valeria could do not to sprint. She was terrified, her heart threatening to pound out of her chest, her pulse thundering in her ears. She shook from head to toe, Turner's warning still echoing in her mind.

"There are eyes everywhere. Don't do anything to draw attention to yourself. Just walk, get on the bus, and call home."

She had been led through a tunnel that came out in the basement of a shop one street over from the embassy. The shopkeeper seemed in on things and had ignored them when they emerged from the back. Turner gave her a hug as if saying goodbye to a friend, then gently pushed her out the door, the bells hanging on the frame chiming, startling her and sending her heart racing.

The bus station wasn't far, and her departure had been timed so she wouldn't wait long for one heading toward her hometown. She turned the corner, breathing a sigh of relief at the sight of buses ahead. She had money in her pocket, provided by Turner—enough to pay for a ticket and food.

She spotted several police officers huddled together at the next street corner. She hesitated. Were they searching for her? If the authorities were hunting her, wouldn't they be watching the bus station? Turner had repeated several times how dangerous it was to leave the protection of the embassy, and Valeria began thinking the woman might have been right.

She forced herself forward, cutting across the street. Cars honked at her, drivers shouting their frustration. She wasn't accustomed to this type of traffic. Back home, there were few cars, mostly farm equipment. If someone honked, it was usually accompanied by a friendly wave and smile.

She glanced out of the corner of her eye and spotted the police turning toward the ruckus, one driver now cursing at her from his window, adding to the chaos. She hurried away, hoping to lose herself in the crowd of pedestrians, when a shout rang out.

"Stop! Police!"

Was it for her? There were hundreds of people within earshot. It could be for anyone, but she had to assume it was for her. She didn't dare look and instead kept walking forward, spotting an alley ahead. She darted into it, glancing over her shoulder just before the darkness swallowed her. Her heart leaped into her throat at the sight of the three police officers rushing across the street, encountering the same traffic she had.

She bolted. Her legs, far shorter than those of the adult men pursuing her, pumped hard. She cleared the alleyway and turned right, heading back toward the embassy. She thought better of it. They would be waiting for her there. She could go back to the shop, but what if they followed her? She could get the shopkeeper in trouble. She could get the Americans in trouble.

She sprinted across the street, this time paying better attention to the traffic, and ducked into yet another alley. Her heart hammered, not just from fear but exertion. The shouts of the police still echoed behind her, though, as far as she could tell, they hadn't gained on her. She turned left out of the alleyway, changing her sprint into a jog, hoping to draw less attention. The last thing she needed was for one of those around her to alert the police.

She recognized a restaurant across the street. Her bus yesterday had taken her right past it. The bus station was to her left, and the restaurant was across the street. It meant the bus she wanted would come right past her, and that should be any minute now. She turned away from the bus station and continued down the street, following the route she assumed the bus home would take, slowing to a brisk walk. Her chest heaved as she resisted the urge to look back. They had recognized her. It had to be her clothing—she was wearing the same clothes as yesterday. She shrugged out of her jacket, folding it up and holding it in front of her. She removed her hat, gripping both with one hand, then unclipped her hair, letting it flow freely. Hopefully, she had changed her appearance enough that the police wouldn't recognize her from behind.

The gears of a bus ground and she stole a glance. The display across the top of the bus sent her heart sprinting once again. It was the bus home. It slowly gained speed, and she prepared herself. It passed, and she darted into the street then reached out, grabbing the handle on the emergency exit, and pulled herself up onto the bumper. She ducked down, hoping no one inside noticed, especially the driver.

And prayed to God no one on the streets cared enough to report her petty crime.

If she could just make it out of the city, she might make it home. She had to warn her family, her uncle, about what had happened before it was too late.

Operations Center 3, CIA Headquarters
Langley, Virginia

Sonya Tong exhaled in frustration. There appeared to be a discrepancy in the Pentagon's system. Two soldiers with the same name—hardly a rare occurrence—had their personnel files mixed up. Their subject, Corporal Diego Mendoza, held prisoner in Venezuela, appeared to be mixed up with another Corporal Diego Mendoza. Somehow, they both had the same service number but different Social Security numbers. They both shared the same birth date but were born in different locations— one Diego Mendoza from Venezuela, the other from Texas.

As far as she could tell, the mix-up occurred when alter-Mendoza transferred to the Pentagon about a week ago. Somebody in personnel must have screwed up, brought up the name rather than the service number, and assumed they were the same person. They had begun applying corrections that made little sense.

But which one is correct?

If their Mendoza's file had been erroneously updated with alter-Mendoza's information, such as birth date, which details were right? She tapped her nose, staring at the screen. She glanced over at Leroux, sitting behind his station, reading something. She sighed. Why couldn't she let it go? What was it about him she found so fascinating?

He still infatuated her, even though they could never be together. She had struggled to get over him, but when she had been shot and nearly died, their true feelings for each other had been revealed. It had brought everything flooding back.

And now?

She couldn't shake it.

She wanted him.

It wasn't a sexual thing—though, of course, she would love to be with him in that way. But to her, a relationship was far more than what happened in the bedroom. Everything she knew about him told her he was the perfect man for her. He wasn't a partier. He wasn't a social animal. And neither was she. Her idea of a good time was curling up on the couch and watching TV or a movie. From conversations over the years, she was well aware that was his idea of a good time as well.

What would it be like to be cuddled in his arms on the couch, watching *The Mandalorian* or some other show? She could only imagine, and, unfortunately, she imagined it far too often.

It was an obsession.

She had even bought herself a Japanese *Dakimakura* body pillow—not one with an anime face or anything ridiculous like that, just a simple shape. She slept with it at night. She would hold it, her legs wrapped around it, squeezing it tight, and imagine it was the love of her life in her arms.

The stuffed creation was comforting. Peaceful. It helped her get to sleep.

She blew air through her lips, staring back at her screen.

God, why didn't I tell him how I felt before Sherrie came along?

She kept blaming herself, yet it wasn't her fault. Sherrie had come along before the obsession. It wasn't until he became her supervisor that she really took notice of him. She had always thought he was cute—a little frumpy, an uber-dork like her—someone she passed in the halls, saw in the cafeteria, but never really knew.

When their boss Morrison promoted him, making him the youngest analyst supervisor in CIA history, and giving him his own team and control of critical ops, she had finally discovered his amazing brain. And that's what attracted her. It wasn't about looks—though he wasn't bad looking at all. It was his mind. How it worked. How he could take disparate pieces of information and find connections no one else could. How he could take world events, seemingly unrelated, and put them together. He was amazing. Unlike anyone she had ever met. And probably ever would again.

She pinched the bridge of her nose, squeezing her eyes shut.

He wasn't for her. He was Sherrie's, an unbelievably sexy, vivacious, exciting spy. How the hell could she ever compete with that? Though she wouldn't. She wasn't the type. She was too shy, too meek, too much of an introvert ever to go after the man she loved when there was another woman involved.

She grunted. Who was she kidding?

Even if Sherrie wasn't involved, she would have never had the courage to tell him how she felt. Yet circumstances beyond her control had changed everything. Now he knew. They both knew. But unless Sherrie got killed on an op, they could never be together since there was no sign those two weren't going the distance.

She couldn't understand it. Those two were polar opposites. The only thing they had in common was the CIA. Other than that, nothing. Sometimes it made her wonder if he was who she thought he was. Maybe alone, in an intimate setting, he was somebody she couldn't stand.

She pursed her lips, staring blankly at her screen.

Maybe he was a completely different person.

She paused.

A completely different person.

She launched a scraping tool and entered parameters for their Mendoza, her heart racing a little at her notion. The software reached out, pulling everything it could find on their man from social media and web searches, sending the data to another monitor. She focused on the photos, her jaw dropping as scores of images appeared.

She tagged one and brought it up. A handsome Latino man stood, saluting the camera in his uniform. His name was on his chest, his unit on his shoulder.

"Holy shit!" she murmured.

Leroux turned. "Found something?"

She wasn't sure yet. She wasn't positive. But if she was right, it changed everything. If she was right, there was something else going on here, something that had to be so highly classified and compartmentalized, there was no way she could share it with Leroux publicly.

Something was going on here.

And she feared what she had just stumbled upon could put them all at risk.

En Route to El Consejo, Venezuela

Valeria shared the bumper with four other people, all around her age. The others had hopped on after the bus had cleared the downtown core of Caracas. It was what she would have done in an ideal situation, but it would have taken her too long to reach the outskirts, not to mention the fact she had no idea how to navigate her way through the capital.

The bus driver appeared fully aware of what they were doing, but had shown no signs he cared. Apparently, his job was to drive, not sweep stowaways off the bumper. She had decided not to spend any of her money. Her mother would know what to do with it when she returned home. One of the other stowaways had a loaf of bread, which he shared with everyone. It settled her rumbling stomach for a short while.

Tension had gripped her the entire trip until she finally began recognizing her surroundings, and when she reached her home, a tremendous wave of relief washed over her. She hopped off the moving bus, calling a quick goodbye to the others, and raced home as fast as she could, avoiding the main streets of her town. The police were undoubtedly searching for her if they had been in Caracas. The last thing she wanted was for them to spot her here. It was one thing to evade the authorities in a big city, but here, there were few places to hide.

The farm was ahead, her uncle's house just to the right. Did she go there first or home? A split-second decision was made, and she bolted to the right, barreling through the open front door.

"Uncle! Uncle! Where are you?"

"Is that you, Valeria?" The voice was weak.

"Yes!" She sped into the living room and found him sitting in his chair, a chair he rarely left these days. He appeared frail, his skin so pale, so sallow. Tears burst forth from her eyes as she fell to her knees. "Uncle, thank God you're home!"

"Where have you been? Your parents have been worried sick."

She collapsed into his arms and he hugged her, but the firm grip she had once known was long gone. "It's terrible! It's terrible!"

"What's terrible, my child?"

"They took Cousin Diego!"

"What?" His voice was suddenly firm, stronger than she had heard in ages.

"They took him yesterday!"

"Tell me everything," he demanded, pushing her away gently and holding her by the shoulders. "Everything."

She relayed the story. How they had walked to the market, how Diego had told her to go home, how the police had arrested him, how the man with the cigar had accused him of being a spy, how she had escaped and headed to the capital, her stay at the embassy, and her return home. Every detail she could remember spilled out, her voice trembling with urgency. Family members began filtering into the room, but she didn't notice. She was too focused on her story, determined to make sure someone knew what had happened.

"And then I came here," she finished, her shoulders slumping, her chest heaving as she caught her breath. Her story was told. She had warned her family, told her uncle what had happened to his son. If something happened to her now, it didn't matter.

Her uncle held out his hand. "Phone."

Her aunt, her cousin's step-mother, rushed forward, placing an odd-looking cellphone in his hand. He quickly dialed a number. "This is Phoenix. I need to speak with you immediately." He ended the call and looked up. "Send the children and grandchildren to the neighbors. Nobody comes back until they hear from me."

Valeria's aunt stood, ushering everyone out of the room.

"What's going on?" Valeria asked, confused by her uncle's sudden transformation.

He held up a finger, already dialing another number. "This is Phoenix. Get over here now."

Three more calls followed, all variations on the same theme.

"Who are you calling?"

"Friends," he replied.

"Friends who can help?"

"Hopefully."

"Do you think they can help Diego?"

Her uncle smiled, patting her cheek. "No. Not people who can help him, but people who can help nonetheless."

She squinted at him. "I don't understand. Your son has been arrested. My cousin has been arrested. Shouldn't we try to help him?"

Her uncle sighed deeply. "My child, there is much going on here that you don't understand."

"Explain it to me! I'm not a child! I went all the way to Caracas! I met with the Americans. I can go back! I can help! I can help save him!"

"My child, my son is perfectly safe."

She stared at him, bewildered. "I don't understand. He was arrested yesterday. Did they set him free?"

He shook his head. "No, my child. My son was never here. The man you call Cousin Diego is a stranger to me. He is not your cousin, and is definitely not my son."

Director Morrison's Office, CIA Headquarters

Langley, Virginia

"I'm sorry, Chris. But I couldn't tell you."

Leroux sat in front of Morrison's desk, still in a state of shock. Normally, he was read in on these things, but this time, he wasn't. Or more accurately, he had been read in, but almost everything he was told was bullshit. Yes, an American citizen had been arrested. That was true. Yes, he had been accused of being a spy. That was true.

Yet nothing else was.

The man wasn't who they had been told he was.

He wasn't sure how he felt. There was a bit of anger there, but he would get over it. The powers that be had their reasons, and apparently, they had decided he didn't need to know what was going on despite his security clearance. He was more hurt, which was childish. He felt betrayed—again, childish. This was a job. His feelings were irrelevant.

"I'm sure you had your reasons, sir."

Morrison leaned forward, clasping his hands and resting his elbows on the desk. "If it were up to me, I would have told you, but once the information reached the president, he compartmentalized it even further than it already was." He smirked. "You weren't supposed to find out. Your people are just too damn good."

Leroux grunted. "You know Sonya. She's like a bloodhound. Once she gets a scent, she doesn't stop until she finds what she's looking for."

"I'll be sure to keep her name out of the report."

Leroux chuckled. "I'm sure she'll appreciate that."

"Does anybody else know?"

"No. Once Sonya realized what she had discovered by accident, she kept it quiet and informed only me. No one else knows."

"And we have to keep it that way for now—unless it becomes operationally necessary to reveal the truth."

"What's the mission, sir?"

"That, I still can't say."

Leroux frowned. "Don't you think I have a need to know?"

Morrison dismissed the concern with a wave of his hand. "No, that's not what I mean. I can't say because I don't know."

Leroux's eyes narrowed. "Now I'm confused."

"Here's what I can tell you," Morrison began. "Two weeks ago, a contact in Venezuela reached out to our newly reopened embassy. It was a message from a source code-named Phoenix. He claimed to have critical intel. Instructions were provided to arrange a meeting using one of our own people. It turns out this leader has an American son."

Leroux leaned back. "Let me guess—Corporal Diego Mendoza, US Army."

"Exactly. One of our assets assumed Corporal Mendoza's identity. A visa was applied for on compassionate grounds, indicating his father, whom he hadn't seen in over a decade, was dying from cancer. It was granted. He was inserted several days ago, exactly as your file indicates. He headed for the real Corporal Mendoza's hometown and made contact with this rebel leader."

"Do we know what this is about?"

"Not yet. Because he had to go in on a commercial flight, he had to go in with no equipment. He registered at the embassy when he arrived, so we know he arrived in-country without any problems, but his orders were to maintain his cover there—even the Chief of Station doesn't know about this. With the embassy newly reopened, we're still sweeping for bugs so couldn't risk it. The next we heard of him was when the young girl reported his arrest. We have no idea what any of this is about, but we have to assume it's serious." Morrison leaned forward. "If this Phoenix—who hasn't been heard of in over a decade—was willing to come out of hiding for it, it must be big."

"But we don't know what."

"There are all kinds of theories flying about—none of them good. And it could all be bullshit."

"What? Just an attempt to get us to fund their cause?"

Morrison clicked through files on his computer. "If we're to believe what the embassy was told, and I quote, 'The intel we have discovered, if not acted upon, could change the strategic balance in this hemisphere.' End quote."

Leroux folded his arms, drumming his fingers. "That sounds ominous."

"Ominous enough that we decided it couldn't be ignored—even if it is all a ruse."

"Any idea how the Venezuelans found out who he was?"

"We're not sure they did. They made an arrest, accused him of being a spy, but that could just be because he's American. When we submitted the visa application, we didn't try to hide his job. If the granting of the visa was an attempt to get their hands on a soldier from the start, why not just arrest him at the airport? They had all his flight information. My guess is something else happened."

"Or he slipped up. Or his contact did."

Morrison inhaled deeply. "Let's hope not. Otherwise, we're screwed."

"So now what's the mission?"

"It hasn't changed. Find him—"

"Which we think we have."

"—guide Delta in, extract him, and get him back stateside so we can find out what he knows."

Leroux nodded. "Delta is about to insert on the Venezuelan coast. We'll get him, sir, and hopefully, this all turns out to have been for nothing."

Morrison grunted. "I hope it is all for nothing, because if it isn't, it means something big is going on, and I never like that—especially in my backyard."

Unknown Location

Venezuela

CIA Operations Officer Rick "Foxglove" Castillo, a.k.a. Corporal Diego Mendoza, sat in the corner of a cell, his eyes shut. One ear was pressed against the cool concrete, providing some relief from the heavy metal blaring from the speakers overhead. His legs were stretched out against the wall, one propped up as his head hung down. His arm was stretched out, blocking his other ear slightly. With his head tilted toward the ground, the glaring lights overhead were muted by his position.

He had discovered that if he simply appeared defeated, they let him be. If he was defiant, they would come in, force him to stand, and make him suffer their tortures. It had been hours since the photograph had been shown to him—a photograph that had surprised him.

He remembered the moment clearly, and at the time, had realized it was a mistake. He had landed in Caracas and met the local contact, friendly hugs exchanged. After all, they were supposed to be family.

Anyone observing his arrival would have thought it was entirely in character.

They had driven from the airport to the town he was supposedly from without interference from the local authorities. But when the old man greeted him, it had been with a handshake, not the warm embrace expected of a father seeing his son for the first time in 15 years.

It should have been harmless—after all, it had taken place inside. But they clearly had the house under surveillance. The photo, taken through a window—perhaps from across the street—was now being used as evidence.

He remembered muttering under his breath to the old man, "Remember, I'm your son," as he forced a smile and embraced him. For the rest of the evening, everything had gone fine. Family from all around came to meet him, and he had remained in character, the ailing old man maintaining the cover as well.

He had gone to bed confident his cover was intact, though he had discovered nothing. There had been no opportunity to talk with his "father" about the intelligence he claimed to have. Day two had been more of the same—family constantly streaming in. When they finally found themselves alone, they had left the house to avoid any possible bugs, and managed a brief five-minute walk before they were joined by Valeria.

"Do you have news of my son?" the old man had asked.

"He's well. We haven't informed him of the situation for security reasons, but I checked on him as I knew you would ask. I'm sure he wishes he could be here."

"As do I, but it's too dangerous. I'm just happy he's safe in America. His mother was right to get him out."

Rick regarded him. "You made a great sacrifice asking me to come in his place. Was it worth it?"

"I think so. Are you aware of what's going on in the jungle?"

Rick had been briefed before leaving—everything they supposedly knew about the Venezuelan regime's activities. There had been nothing alarming, nothing that could affect the strategic balance like the man claimed. But he had to play it right. "Why don't you tell me what's going on in the jungle?"

The old man smirked. "Clever. Never reveal what you know or what you don't know. Very well. Information has come my way that there's a significant undertaking in the jungle not far from here."

"What kind of undertaking?"

"That's for you to find out. We've noticed an unusual number of transports on the river—far more than usual. They're offloading less than ten kilometers south on the east bank. If you head down the river, you won't be able to miss it. They've built a dock to handle the increased traffic and cut a road into the jungle. Something big is going on."

"How long has this been happening?"

"Almost two months. We noticed the dock go up a couple of months ago, then saw the road being cut. Three weeks ago, the shipping traffic increased dramatically."

"Do you know what kind of cargo?"

"Personnel and equipment. It's definitely army-related, no doubt about that. This isn't a civilian project."

"The Venezuelan army isn't exactly a threat to the United States."

"If it's what we suspect, it definitely could be."

"And what do you suspect?"

"This isn't a Venezuelan operation."

The door to the cell swung open, ending Rick's reverie, just as Valeria's arrival had cut off their conversation. His interrogator stood in the doorway, cigar firmly in place. The man reached outside the cell and switched off the music, dimming the lights.

Rick rose to his feet. "Could you put the music back on, please? Cannibal Corpse is one of my favorite bands. Reminds me of a concert I saw in Jersey."

The interrogator bristled, clearly frustrated by his lack of success. "You think you're clever, don't you? But you've revealed yourself."

Rick leaned into the corner, folding his arms. "Oh?"

"You're far too calm for someone in your position."

"Perhaps I'm simply projecting a calm demeanor."

"Which again reveals who you truly are," the man shot back.

Rick sighed. "Listen. I've told you who I am. You know who I am. I've told you why I'm here. All the paperwork was submitted through your embassy. I didn't try to hide the fact I was coming here. I didn't hide my job. I'm a corporal. I work at the Pentagon. I just make sure the brass gets fed. I'm a nobody. I'm just here to see my father before he dies."

The interrogator leaned in. "How did you know to come?"

Rick was ready for this question. "I got an email from a cousin in Florida."

"And how did this cousin find out?"

"I have no idea. I didn't ask. All I cared about was that my father was dying."

The photograph was held up again. "And yet you're still unwilling to explain this."

"Explain what?" Rick said evenly. "A father hasn't seen his son in over fifteen years. Instead of embracing him, he shakes his hand. You obviously have good intel. I assume you heard the conversation. I assume you saw what happened next."

"What do you mean?"

"I assume you have additional photographs."

"Of course."

"And what do they show?"

Silence.

"I'll tell you what they show. They show an old man, dying, who just shook the hand of someone he didn't realize was his son. And then, when it was made clear to him, he embraced him joyfully. You know that. You've got the photographs. If you've got that one, you've got the others."

The interrogator took a long puff of his cigar then exhaled several impressive smoke rings. "This is true. That's exactly what the photographs show. Except for one thing you're leaving out."

"And what's that?"

"We also have listening devices in the house. Are you going to say what we heard? Or shall I?"

Rick tensed, but hid it well—or so he hoped. "I'm all ears."

The cigar was removed, and the interrogator smiled. "'Remember, I'm your son.'"

North of Venezuelan Coast

Dawson stepped off the Black Hawk and plunged toward the water below. The seas were calm, which would make their trip to the coastline easier. However, the calm necessitated a drop farther out. Choppy seas would have impeded not only their line of sight, but also coastal radar detection close to sea level. With the water calm, they couldn't risk being spotted.

He hit the water, sinking below the surface before a few kicks brought his head back above the waves. Drawing a breath, he spotted the inflatable bobbing nearby and headed for it. It had taken most of the day to get here. While the distance looked close on a map, maps were notoriously inaccurate in their portrayals of what the world truly looked like. Professor Acton had explained once that Western prejudices maintained the distortion created by mapmaker Gerardus Mercator half a millennium before. While it was useful for naval navigation at the time, the distorted enlargement of Europe and North America was no longer necessary. Ships no longer navigated using this system. Not to mention the fact that, contrary to a far too common popular belief, the world was not flat—it was round, leaving North Carolina and the Venezuelan coast, in reality, quite far apart.

Yet none of that mattered. They would have waited until dark regardless.

He rolled over the side and into the Combat Rubber Raiding Craft, two CRRCs, carried underslung by the Black Hawk, deployed only minutes ago. He pushed to his knees and surveyed the area as the chopper overhead banked away, its job done, the pilot continuing to hug the deck. It was essential to ensuring the Venezuelans didn't know they were coming. Stealth was their only hope of rescuing their target.

Dawson had mixed feelings about the mission. Rescuing idiots who ventured into war zones unnecessarily seemed like a waste of resources. Yet someone further up the food chain disagreed, and their orders were clear. Somebody in Washington had decided risking their lives was worth it. His job wasn't to question his orders or the wisdom of the brass in the government he served. His job was to execute the orders handed to him and react on the ground in real time to whatever didn't go according to plan.

He flipped down his night vision goggles and spotted Red in the second boat. His friend gave him a wave, his goggles already in place.

"Give a lady a hand."

Dawson turned to see Niner grabbing on to the side of the boat. He hauled him in, and Atlas soon followed, rocking them furiously. Spock, Mickey, and Angus joined them, then Atlas manned the outboard motor, steering them south. Dawson checked to see Red's boat hanging back.

They would head out ten minutes behind them. Two boats together were more likely to be spotted than one alone.

He took a seat, leaning against the gunwale and flipping up his night vision goggles. He blinked rapidly, the quarter moon overhead obscured by mostly cloudy skies, barely allowing him to make out the rest of the team, already chit-chatting to kill the time.

"According to Vanessa, the Atlas burger was a hit," said Spock.

The newest team member, Sergeant Gary "Angus" Tye, raised a finger. "I had one. It was awesome."

Niner agreed. "What's not to love? Three all-beef patties, three-quarters of a pound of beef, three types of bacon, three types of cheese, grilled onions and mushrooms, and that sauce!" He kissed the tips of his fingers. "Magnifico!" He swatted Atlas' chest. "A huge chunk of cow meat named after a huge chunk of man meat."

Atlas swatted Niner much harder. "Don't you start."

Niner rubbed his shoulder in exaggerated pain. "I don't need to be tenderized, big man."

Dawson couldn't see the eye roll, but he was certain Atlas had given one.

"All kidding aside, Vanessa's All American Food Truck better work out, or I won't be retiring until I'm sixty-five," said Atlas.

Niner raised an eyebrow. "What do you mean?"

"I mean, I'm footing the bill for this entire operation. Don't tell her I told you. She didn't want anybody to know, but we don't keep secrets in the Unit."

Spock cocked an eyebrow. "Odd, I thought that's exactly what we did."

Atlas flipped him the bird, and Spock reached over, slapping the big man on the leg. "Just kidding, brother. That's gotta be stressful."

"You have no idea. Do you realize how hard it is to save any amount of money on a sergeant's salary?"

Spock grunted. "Preaching to the choir, brother. I think taxpayers believe that since they give us free clothing and feed us while we're on duty, we don't deserve to be paid well."

Dawson had to agree. Life was tough in the military, and his team had things better than many, getting extra pay for what they did. What Atlas had done proved he loved and had faith in his partner, but that only got you so far. "Has she got a location?"

Atlas nodded. "Yeah, just off base. Should be close enough to get military traffic and civilian traffic to boot. If it works out, the ultimate goal, of course, is to get her own restaurant. She wants to do that within five years."

"Or she could become a food truck queen," said Niner. "That food was damn good."

Dawson agreed. "It was fantastic, and the colonel loved his wrap, and I know Maggie enjoyed the hell out of helping her out."

"I hear the restaurant business is brutal," said Angus. "In today's age, online reviews…well, you know, can be vicious."

"That woman's got a thick skin. She's tough. I think she can take it," said Atlas. "But if anybody hurts her feelings online, I'm calling in some favors from Langley to find out who the hell they are." He held up two meaty fists.

"That's one of the biggest problems with the damn Internet—anonymity."

Spock grunted. "You'll get no argument from me. My daughter's been dealing with some issues. Anonymous posts saying horrible things about her mother."

Dawson bristled. "What are you talking about?"

Spock waved a hand. "Don't worry about it. I'm dealing with it. But it just pisses me off that anybody can say anything on the Internet with no consequences. There should be a law that requires any site that allows you to post, to verify identity. Doesn't mean you can't post anonymously, but if you say something slanderous, libelous, or hateful—something that violates the law—you should be able to sue. Get their actual name and address. If they knew they could get their face punched in or lose their house for posting some of that bullshit on the Internet, maybe they'd think twice."

Dawson sighed. "Yeah, the Internet is an amazing thing, and I think the world is better off because of it, but in some ways, we're far worse off. Parts of it have turned into a cesspool. That's why I spend as little time as I can on social media."

Sergeant Trip "Mickey" McDonald agreed. "You and me both. I don't have an account anywhere. I look stuff up on the Internet if I need to. I'll read the news from reputable sites. But no Facebook, no Twitter, or whatever the hell they call it these days. No nothing. Never saw the point, never will."

Angus disagreed. "Oh, I don't know. I use it to keep in touch with people from high school, from basic. If you keep the politics out of it, it's good. Just make sure you never like a post that's even remotely controversial, report misinformation, and block anyone who really pisses you off. I don't need that crap in my life."

"Neither does my daughter," said Spock. "My God, kids today are cruel. I'm not saying they weren't when we were kids, but holy hell, it's reached a whole new level, especially now with the social media. I'd hate to be a kid today. From the moment you wake up to the moment you sleep, you're jacked into everything. Life is at hyper-speed. These kids are expected to put everything they do online, and if they don't get likes, they're crushed."

"It's absolutely ridiculous," Dawson said, his head bobbing in agreement. "Sometimes it makes me wonder whether Maggie and I should bring a kid into this world. It's so screwed up."

Spock's eyebrow cocked. "You two thinking of having a kid?"

"That was always the plan. The question was the timing. Something tells me with the direction things are heading, world peace isn't on the horizon."

"No shit," muttered Angus. "I think you'll be gainfully employed for quite a while."

"Well, no one said I had to fight *all* the wars. I don't want to leave the Unit, and Maggie doesn't expect me to. But, as we know, anything could happen."

Spock, a recent widower, sighed. "Anything can happen, BD. And it doesn't have to happen to you. It could happen to Maggie."

Dawson regarded the man, his grief still palpable. They were all still grieving. Spock's wife had been out shopping for dresses with Maggie for the wedding when she had been shot. Life was cruel. The innocent always got hurt, even on the streets of America. Maggie had been shot once, though that hadn't been here at home, and it certainly wasn't an innocent situation. He sighed. "You're right. The world's probably never going to get better."

"And don't forget," Angus added, "it's always sucked."

Dawson chuckled. "They keep telling us the fifties were good."

"I always thought we were heading in the right direction, but not anymore," said Spock. "There's no point holding off, hoping things will get better. The decision has to be based on when it's the right time for both of you."

"Maybe just let nature decide," suggested Niner. "Switch her birth control for Tic Tacs."

Dawson gave him a look. "I think maybe she'd like to participate in the decision."

"Probably would. I withdraw my suggestion." Niner's eyebrows shot up. "And stop withdr—"

Atlas reached forward and smacked him. "Don't you dare say it." The big man gestured ahead from his position manning the motor. "There's the coast."

Dawson rose and flipped his night vision goggles back into place. A dim light, invisible moments before, was now clearly visible, the coded pattern indicating it was their contact. "You see him?"

"Yes," rumbled Atlas, adjusting their heading slightly.

"Let's hope this isn't a Charlie-Foxtrot, boys. I got babies to make."

Unknown Location

Venezuela

Rick Castillo suppressed his surprise, the surveillance of his "father" far more extensive than expected. He tilted his head to the side and smirked. "Sounds like something from a Telenovela."

The interrogator's grin widened, his satisfaction at the perceived victory evident. He slowly paced in front of Rick, the cigar held like a weapon, its smoldering tip leaving faint trails of smoke in the stale air. "We know you're not who you say you are. The question is, who are you really?"

Rick shrugged. "I already told you. Corporal. Pentagon. Lunch guy. It's not exactly riveting, but it's the truth."

The interrogator barked a laugh, his voice echoing in the small cell. "You think this is a game? You think you can walk out of here with clever quips and a shrug?"

"Honestly? No. But what you think you know and what is true are two very different things. If you're convinced I'm a threat, then you'll keep me here. If you're not, you'll let me go. Either way, I'm done explaining myself."

The man's amusement vanished in an instant, replaced by a steely glare. "You think we're stupid? You think we can't see through your little charade? But don't worry, you'll tell us everything. One way or another." He turned sharply, his boots scraping against the concrete as he left the cell. The heavy door slammed shut behind him, the reverberation echoing in Rick's ears, replaced moments later by the din of heavy metal, the lights returning to their full intensity.

Rick exhaled slowly, his mind racing. The old man had slipped up, but so had he. He shouldn't have said what he had. He should have assumed he was under heavy surveillance. It was an amateur move, and he was better than that.

And his screw up might just cost him his life.

SEBIN Black Site

San Miguel, Venezuela

Alejandro Torres, their local contact, pointed ahead. "That's your target."

Dawson peered through his binoculars, scanning down the road toward the SEBIN compound. It was well lit, with no attempt to conceal its presence. "They certainly aren't trying to hide that they're there. What can you tell me about it?"

The contact pursed his lips. "Not much. Usually, if you go in there, you never come out. And the few that do are broken men. They rarely talk. The only thing I can tell you is that, if the person you're looking for is there, they're in the basement."

"The basement?"

"The one thing everyone agrees on. When they arrive, they're taken down steps and never see a window the entire time they're there, even when they're moved between rooms."

"How many personnel?"

"No idea. You've got four at the main gate, four towers at the corners with two men in each, and a roving dog patrol on the inside. Everything else is hidden away. I couldn't tell you if there are five people inside the building or a hundred-and-five. It's not wise to hang around here. Can't you guys just park a satellite overhead? Use infrared?"

"That's not exactly how it works." Dawson fell back to where Red and the rest of the breach team waited. "Okay, boys, our target is most likely in the basement. Security appears exactly as we were briefed. Four at the main gate, four towers at the corners with two men each, one roving dog patrol, and an unknown number of hostiles inside. We'll stick with the original plan, and hopefully, by the time they realize we're there, we'll be on our way out." He turned to Red. "Your guys will be covering our six. We're coming out the number two side. You'll pick us up and we'll head down the back street to the rendezvous point. You provide cover, take out anything pursuing us, and then we get out of town like a bat out of hell to the exfil point at the river. Understood?"

"We've got you covered."

"Good." Dawson turned to his team. "Set?"

"Yes, Sergeant Major," his men echoed.

Niner grinned at Red. "Dawson and Maggie are gonna start making babies."

Red's eyebrows shot up. "So, you guys made the decision?"

Dawson gave them both a look. "Do you really think this is the time to discuss this?"

Red shrugged. "I didn't bring it up."

Dawson turned to Torres. "Are you sure you're up for this?"

"Absolutely," replied Torres.

"Good." Dawson jerked his chin toward the nearby car they had commandeered. "Then let's get to it." He activated his comms. "Control, this is Zero-One. We're ready at this end, over."

"Zero-One, Control Actual. Copy that. Drone is in position. Give us the word, and the power's down, over."

"Roger that, Control. Stand by." Dawson gave a thumbs-up to Torres, now behind the wheel. The young man returned the gesture. He couldn't be issued comms in case something went wrong and he was searched. He shouldn't need them if things went according to plan. A bottle of hooch was pulled from a bag on the passenger seat. Torres took several swigs, then poured some on his hands, rubbing it onto his face and chest. He needed to reek of alcohol if the plan was to work.

Dawson turned to the others. "Everyone in position. We go in sixty seconds." He headed back toward the corner as Red sprinted away. "Bravo Team, Zero-One. Confirm in position, over."

Reports came in from the others, confirming everyone was at their assigned stations. He turned to the assault team made up of Niner, Atlas, Spock, Mickey, and Angus. "Ready?"

They all nodded.

"Good. Then let's do this." He activated his comms again. "This is Zero-One. Sending in diversion now." He gave Torres a thumbs-up. The engine roared to life, the car surging forward and hanging a sharp right, barreling toward the main gate as it swerved from side to side, the radio blaring Paradise City, the bottle of booze waving out the window.

Niner peered around the corner. "I get the distinct impression he's done this before."

Atlas grinned. "I think we'll have to talk to the young man about the dangers of drinking and driving after we're done."

The car swerved hard to the left, crashing into the front gate. Shouts erupted. Dawson peered through his binoculars to see all eyes, even from the guard towers, now focused on the commotion.

"Control, Zero-One. Take out the power."

"Zero-One, Control. Taking out the power. Stand by."

Torres threw the car into reverse, ramming it into a power pole. Sparks flew overhead, and the town went dark as Langley's drone detonated a mini-EMP over the power lines leading into the town, temporarily disabling them.

"This is Zero-One. Execute, execute, execute!"

Rick sat in the corner as he had for hours. The music still blared, the lights still glared, yet it all went unnoticed. He had tuned it out, absorbed instead by the discovery he had been made. The Venezuelans didn't know who or what he was, though he was certain they suspected he was CIA or some equivalent. They certainly knew he wasn't who he claimed to be.

What didn't make sense to him was the level of surveillance on the man codenamed Phoenix. His briefing had indicated Phoenix hadn't been active in over a decade. So why did they have such intense surveillance set up on him? There was no way they would maintain that level for so long if he was truly out of the game. And if he wasn't, as was apparently the case, it was hard to believe they would have let Phoenix operate actively for so long without intervening.

It had to be related to his arrival. The visa paperwork had indicated his destination and who he was meeting with. Had the Venezuelans set up surveillance on the house just in case something untoward was occurring? It was a definite possibility, despite the solid cover. The man was dying, and the Venezuelans had never shown an interest in repatriating former citizens who had escaped the regime as children. He couldn't see them risking an international incident simply because his cover was an American soldier.

Though it wouldn't be the first time.

His mission was toast unless he could get out of there. Something was going on in the jungle, and Langley had to be made aware so they could send a team in to determine exactly what. As much as he would love to lead that team, the likelihood of that was next to nothing. He had to get a message out, though right now, he couldn't see any way. Since arriving, he had seen only his cell, an interrogation room, and the corridor in between. That was it.

He had seen his interrogator and two guards. Cigar Man would be loyal. There would be no compromising him. And it was hard to compromise two guards together. If he found himself alone with one, he could make an offer they couldn't refuse, but he had to make it as easy as possible for them to comply.

"Give me a pen and paper, and I'll have a million bolivars delivered to you within a week."

It might be enough to tempt someone. After all, what harm could come from writing materials? Then the note could be pressed into a palm—a message to be delivered to a dead drop already set up—with the promise of another five million. It was doable if he survived long enough, and if he could just get that one weak soul alone with him.

All he needed was 30 seconds.

The music abruptly cut off and the lights flickered out, plunging him into absolute darkness. Shouts from the other side of the metal door revealed surprise, with a hint of panic. Heavy footfalls echoed down the corridor.

He pushed to his feet, staring into the darkness, finally picking out a dim rectangle of light around the edge of the door. Light still shone in the corridor, though the confusion continued, indicating it wasn't simply an end to his torture. Something else was happening.

He glanced up into the corner to his right. The red light of the camera monitoring him was as dead as those overhead. He groped his way toward it then reached up, finding the cable connecting the camera to the main system. He yanked it free, cutting the feed should the power be restored. They would be blind and forced to come into the cell, which might give him an opportunity to surprise them. He had no idea what was going on. It could just be a power blackout—the grid wasn't exactly reliable in this failing state. But it could also be an attempt at rescue, and he had to be prepared.

He pressed his ear against the door and waited, praying Langley had sent someone to save his ass.

Dawson peered through his binoculars, watching the 1-2 corner tower, smiling as both guards dropped, Red's team going to work. Reports came in over his comms indicating all four towers had been secured.

"This is Zero-One, breaching now," he said, darting across the street.

At the front gate, Torres backed the car up yet again, reversing into a parked car. He was putting on a good show, but it was going on too long. He was supposed to run into the gate, back up into the pole so there was a believable explanation for the power outage, then leave. He was going to get himself killed, and he wasn't on comms to be warned to knock it off.

Dawson reached the wall, cupping his hands. Spock stepped into them with a boot, and Dawson hoisted him to the top. Spock straddled it and reached down, hauling Dawson up. Dawson dropped to the ground, taking a knee as he quickly surveyed the area while Spock continued to pull the rest of the team over the wall. Niner then Atlas dropped beside him, and he indicated the dog patrol—the K9 and its master rushing toward the commotion at the front gate.

The generator roared to life and the compound lights flickered back on, though dimmer than before. They were still hidden by the shadows cast by the now-unmanned guard tower. Unfortunately, they apparently stank. The German shepherd strained against its leash, its nose aimed directly at Dawson's team.

Dawson raised his M4 but held his fire. He wasn't taking out a dog unless innocent lives were at stake, and taking out its master would mean a loose leash, turning the beast into a danger. He pulled a device from his utility belt and pressed the button, activating an extremely high-pitched noise audible only to the dog. It immediately lowered its head to the ground, whimpering and raising its paws in an attempt to cover its ears. Dawson left the device on the ground then put two rounds into the handler.

He indicated the advance, and Niner took point as they raced across the walled compound, reaching the generator along the side of the lone building as gunfire broke out at the main gate. They reached the generator without being discovered, and Spock cut the fuel line, sending diesel gushing onto the concrete. The generator sputtered, then fell silent, the lights dimming and plunging them into darkness once again.

Atlas fit a small charge on the side door their intelligence indicated led to the basement where the prisoners were held. The lock blew, and Atlas hauled the door open as gunfire erupted at the front gate.

"Niner, take point," ordered Dawson. Niner headed inside, followed by Atlas and Spock. Dawson turned to Mickey and Angus. "Cover our sixes. Try not to shoot us on our way out."

Mickey grinned. "I make no promises."

Dawson headed down the stairs into the darkness below as Red delivered an update.

"This is Zero-Two. Torres has been taken out. No signs of life, over."

"Copy that," replied Dawson, the news disappointing but expected—Torres hadn't followed orders. Dawson reached the bottom of the stairs and turned a corner to find a corridor stretching out ahead of them. The dim emergency lighting barely illuminated the length of the hall, lined with metal doors on both sides—clearly prison cells.

Their contact's intel had been solid so far. They would mourn the young man's passing, but there was no time for that now. They had to achieve their mission and make their extraction point before the Venezuelans had time to react.

Niner's suppressed M4 belched lead ahead. Two shots, and a target dropped at the far end of the hallway as he continued to advance. Any resistance would come from that end of the hall, and they had no idea how strong that resistance might be—but it would grow stronger the longer they were here. They didn't have time to search every cell.

"Corporal Diego Mendoza! Identify yourself!" Dawson shouted, resulting in a cocked eyebrow from Spock. Dawson shrugged. "Can you think of a quicker way?"

Somebody hammered on a cell door ahead. Atlas spun, pointing at it. Dawson jogged over and rapped on the door. "Mendoza?"

"Yes! I'm here!" came a voice.

"What was the lunch special last Tuesday?" Dawson demanded, Langley assuring him their target would know.

Laughing, the voice replied, "Meatloaf with mashed potatoes and green beans."

"That's him." Dawson stepped back as Atlas slid the locking bar aside and yanked the door open. Their target stepped out, appearing as if he hadn't been worked over too badly. "Can you walk?"

"Absolutely."

Dawson jerked a thumb over his shoulder. "Get your ass up those stairs. Two of my men are at the top."

"You've got it."

More gunfire erupted from Niner's position, the resistance stiffening as expected.

"Fall back! We've got our man!" ordered Dawson.

Niner didn't acknowledge but halted his advance. The gunfire intensified, though it was random and unaimed. Dawson added his own firepower, as did Atlas, flanking Niner as they all fell back toward the stairwell.

Something clanged, and Dawson cursed at the familiar sound.

"Grenade!" shouted Niner as he rushed forward and kicked out before turning and ducking as a horrific explosion erupted, shaking the entire structure, Dawson's Sonic Defender earplugs the only thing saving him from permanent hearing damage. He pushed to his knees, spinning back to see the ceiling collapsed on Niner's position.

"Niner!" cried Atlas, the fear for his friend clear in his voice as the big man rushed toward the rubble.

Dawson scrambled forward, Spock at his side, as Atlas tore at the debris. "Do you have him?"

Atlas continued to toss aside pieces of the collapsed ceiling before crying out in relief. "I've got him!"

Dawson glanced at Niner's unmoving form as he advanced past him, continuing to pour fire at the other end of the hallway. "Is he alive?"

"I don't know."

"Get him, and let's get the hell out of here. We'll figure it out up top." Dawson didn't bother checking on Atlas' progress, instead focusing on the job ahead.

"I've got him!"

"Fall back!" ordered Dawson as he and Spock continued to provide suppression fire. Another explosion rocked the basement, this grenade not tossed far, the damage closer to the opposition's end.

"Debris!" warned Spock as they reached the collapsed ceiling. Spock climbed over the rubble, covering Dawson as he scrambled over the pile, and they both continued to retreat.

"We're clear!" shouted Atlas from the entrance to the stairwell. They hastened their exit, reaching the stairwell, and Spock sprinted up after Atlas and Niner.

Dawson followed, taking the steps two at a time and emerging into the night. He activated his comms. "We have our target. One-One down—I repeat, One-One down!"

"Copy that, Zero-One," replied an emotionless Red. "Moving into position now. ETA thirty seconds. Taking out the main gate."

Gunfire crackled, and the activity at the main gate fell silent.

"Gate secured," reported Red as engines roared on the other side of the wall.

They reached their exit point, and Spock boosted Mickey to the top. Mickey straddled the wall and reached down, grabbing Niner's lifeless form and pulling it up beside him. Angus and Spock followed, dropping to the other side as Mickey lowered Niner into their arms. Their target then Atlas climbed the wall with boosts from Dawson, then Mickey hauled him up. They both dropped to the other side just as Red and Sergeant Zack "Wings" Hauser arrived in their prearranged rides. Everyone piled in, Dawson taking the passenger seat beside Red.

"Let's get the hell out of here!"

"You don't have to ask me twice." Red floored it, sending them careening down the road away from the compound, Wings stopping at the corner to pick up the rest of the covering team. Dawson twisted in his seat to find Atlas performing chest compressions on Niner.

"Status?" Dawson demanded.

Spock shook his head as he hooked up a defibrillator. "No pulse."

Dawson cursed, turning to their target. "You better have been worth it."

Operations Center 3, CIA Headquarters

Langley, Virginia

Leroux stood in the middle of the operations center, hands clasped behind his back as he took in the scene on multiple screens. Body cams, drone footage, and satellite feeds displayed personnel pouring out of the compound's lone structure. Garage doors opened, and four vehicles rushed out, the first bursting through the damaged main gate, heading after Dawson and his team. He glanced at a map showing a Black Hawk and two AH-64 Apaches crossing the Coastal Mountain Range, hugging the deck and avoiding population centers, though the noise would be impossible to conceal.

"ETA for those choppers?" he asked.

"Nine minutes," replied Tong, tapping at her keyboard, the projected routes of the helicopters and Bravo Team appearing on the display.

"Status on One-One?"

Tong's eyes glistened. "It doesn't look good."

He cursed. "Get me a secure channel with the target."

"Stand by," Tong replied. "Zero-One, Control. We need the target on comms, over."

Dawson's voice came through, all business despite the underlying concern for his comrade. "Stand by, Control."

"I'm on comms," said their target a moment later.

"Secure this channel," ordered Leroux, fitting his headset into place and sitting at his station. Tong gave a thumbs-up.

"Foxglove, this is Control Actual. Confirm your identity. Validation code Alpha-Alpha-One-Four-One-Tango, over."

"Authorization code recognized. This is Foxglove. Code X-ray-Zulu-Seven-Two-Nine-Seven-Charlie, over."

Leroux checked the code against his file. "Identity confirmed. Report, over."

"Contact was made. Phoenix reports unusual activity on the river about ten klicks south of his position. Apparently, a dock has been built, and there's frequent river traffic unloading military equipment and personnel, using a road cut into the jungle within the past two months."

"Do you have any evidence supporting Phoenix's claim?"

"Negative. I need to go down that road and see what the hell's at the end of it."

"Negative, Foxglove. Your orders are to return for a full debrief."

"Debrief on what? I don't know anything! All I have is a location."

Leroux muted his mic and turned to Tong. "Look for a newly constructed dock with a road into the jungle, approximately ten klicks south of the original arrest point."

"I'm on it," Tong replied.

Leroux unmuted. "Your orders are to return with the team."

"People have died," snapped Foxglove. "We need to know why. There's something more going on here—something big—and it's not controlled by the Venezuelans."

This piqued Leroux's interest. "If it's not local, then who is it?"

"The old man didn't get a chance to say. I was arrested before I could get more from him. They had eyes and ears on him. I could tell he was scared. One thing he made clear—it will affect the strategic balance in the hemisphere. I'm not leaving until I find out what the hell is actually going on."

The door to the operations center hissed open, and Morrison entered.

"Stand by, Foxglove," said Leroux, muting his mic again.

"Status?" asked Morrison.

"We've got him, but they're being pursued. Foxglove says there's something going on in the jungle south of Phoenix's location. He's requesting permission to pursue it. It sounds like it's not a Venezuelan operation, but a foreign one."

Morrison's eyebrows shot up, and he cursed. "Foreign? Do we have another Cuban Missile Crisis here?"

"I don't know," replied Leroux, pointing at the display. "But they're barely going to make it out of this, if they make it out at all. Niner's apparently KIA."

Morrison cursed again. "If this is a foreign operation, we have to know. Tell Foxglove he's a go."

"What about Bravo Team?"

"They're too damn big to hide. The Venezuelans have to think they got away. I want them out, but Foxglove can stay."

"Yes, sir." Leroux unmuted his mic. "Foxglove, Control Actual. You're clear to remain behind. Equip yourself with comms and gear and prepare to separate from the group, over."

"Roger that, Control. Foxglove, out."

"Keep me posted," ordered Morrison as he headed for the exit, the door hissing shut behind him.

Leroux sat, all eyes on him, but he ignored them. Only he and Tong knew what was really going on, and for now, it had to stay that way.

San Miguel, Venezuela

"What the hell is going on?" asked Dawson, having only been privy to one side of their target's conversation. "Who the hell are you?"

"I'm not at liberty to say."

"You're not at liberty?" Dawson glared at the man, jabbing a finger at Niner. "I just lost one of my best friends. Just who the hell are you? There's no way in hell you're Corporal Mendoza. You're CIA!"

"Clear!" shouted Mickey and Atlas leaned back, the portable defibrillator zapping Niner as gunfire rattled behind them.

Niner bolted upright, gasping for air, his eyes wide and his mouth open. "What the hell just happened?"

Atlas grabbed him, hugging him hard then pushing him back, gripping his shoulders and shaking him. "You're alive!"

"No shit," said Niner, glancing down to see his bare chest and the leads attached to it. He turned to Mickey. "Did you zap me?"

"Yeah. Want to do it again?"

Niner grinned. "Oh yeah. I feel alive!"

Wings interrupted over the comms. "This is One-Two. We're taking heavy fire back here. Permission to engage with something a little heavier, over."

"One-Two, Zero-One. Permission granted, over." Dawson reached over and gave Niner's shoulder a smack. "Good to have you back, brother." He leaned out the window to see a round from a Carl Gustav 84mm recoilless rifle launch from Wings' ride. One of their pursuers erupted in flames moments later, the explosion silhouetting the wreckage against the night as it lifted several feet into the air before crashing back to the ground and flipping multiple times. The SUV behind it slammed into the wreck, taking two of their four pursuers out of the equation.

Dawson returned his attention to Foxglove. "What's going on? Why are you here?"

"If you have to ask, then you haven't been read in. Your job was to get me out. Now I have to complete my job."

"Which is?"

"To find out what the hell's going on in the jungle south of where I was arrested."

"That's not our mission. Our mission is to get you out and onto the chopper. I don't know if you're aware of this, but you're hours away from where you were arrested. There's no way you're getting back there alone."

"Then come with me."

"I can't. Those aren't my orders."

"Screw orders. Sometimes you just have to do what's right."

Dawson cursed, activating his comms. "Control Actual, this is Zero-One. Read me in. Now!"

"Stand by, Zero-One."

"What's going on, BD?" Red asked, still driving.

"I don't know yet, but I have a feeling this mission is far from over."

The Unit

Fort Liberty, North Carolina

Maggie flinched at Clancy's phone slamming into the cradle, followed by a string of angry curses interspersed with strongly worded opinions on the CIA. She rose from her desk and poked her head into his office, tapping gently on the doorframe.

"Is everything okay?"

An angry Clancy growled. "This mission is turning into a Charlie Foxtrot."

Maggie tensed, fully aware the call had been about the mission her husband and friends were on. "Did something go wrong?"

Clancy inhaled deeply, holding his breath, then leaned back in his chair and gestured for Maggie to sit. She took a seat in front of his desk, her hands trembling.

"They're heading to their exfil point now. They successfully achieved their mission objective. Just so you know, because rumors will start flying, we lost Niner—"

She gasped, but he quickly held up a hand.

"For a few minutes. He's fine. I guess his heart stopped or something after a grenade detonated near him. They revived him. But I've just been informed that who we were told the target was, actually isn't."

She stared at him, confused. "I don't understand."

He sighed again, waving his hand. "Doesn't matter. Everything I just said is classified. All I can say is, don't expect them home for dinner." He pointed toward the door. "Shut it on the way out. I've got some calls to make."

"Yes, sir." She rose and closed the door, returning to her desk, her entire body shaking as she replayed the conversation. They had achieved their objective—that was good. They were heading to the exfil point—also good. But Clancy was pissed about something, and his statement, "Don't expect them home for dinner," suggested that until now, they had been expected home for dinner—and now weren't.

Something had changed. And while she wasn't privy to what he knew—whatever was going on and what had changed weren't things she needed to know—this job gave her information none of the other spouses had, which was both a blessing and a curse. Her friends were at home or at work, blissfully ignorant of everything their partners did. She, on the other hand, often knew exactly what was going on—or, like today, knew just enough to worry.

She clasped her trembling hands together and stared up at the heavens.

Please, God, take care of them. They may be men of war, but they're doing your work.

San Miguel, Venezuela

Dawson listened intently as Leroux brought him up to speed on what was actually happening. It had taken a couple of minutes to get permission to read him in on a secure channel, and he wasn't liking what he was hearing.

The entire mission had been a lie.

The man they had rescued wasn't a US Army corporal at all. He was a CIA operations officer designated "Foxglove," sent to receive intel from a rebel leader codenamed "Phoenix." From what Dawson gathered, something was indeed going on in the jungle, something big, and a foreign power was behind it. This was too big to ignore. It could be the Chinese, the Russians, or even the Iranians or North Koreans.

Whatever was going on, they had to know.

Dawson glanced at Niner, who was once again dressed with his body armor back in place. Despite being recently revived, he was downing his second bottle of water and cracking jokes with the others, apparently none the worse for wear.

If there was indeed something going on in the jungle that involved America's enemies, they couldn't risk sending just one man. Foxglove needed backup.

Dawson cut off Leroux. "Requesting change in mission. We'll be remaining with Foxglove."

"Zero-One, repeat your last, over."

"You heard me. We're staying with Foxglove." The statement ended all conversations, everyone staring at him.

"Negative, Zero-One. Your orders stand."

"If what you say is true, this is too important. He needs backup."

"If backup is required, then it will be sent in later."

"Negative, Control. We're here now, on the ground. We'll do it so another team doesn't have to. Besides, our mission was to extract him, and until his ass is out of Venezuelan territory, we haven't accomplished our mission."

A burst of static from Leroux's end indicated a heavy sigh. "Stand by, Zero-One."

"Copy that."

Another explosion behind them indicated that Wings' team had successfully taken out the last of their pursuers. For the moment, they were free and clear, and this was the time for tactics to change.

"What the hell's going on, BD?" Red asked from the driver's seat.

Dawson glanced at Foxglove. "I'm not entirely sure yet." He turned to the others. "As I'm sure you've probably gathered from what you've overheard, our friend here is CIA, and there just might be something happening in the jungle that needs to be checked out—something that can apparently affect the strategic balance in this hemisphere. Something that might be foreign-controlled."

Niner cursed. "Those damn Canadians. I always knew they were a threat."

Atlas snorted. "Yeah, with their forty-four pounds of fentanyl coming over the border, and that maple syrup? It's been invading American waistlines for decades. We should definitely invade."

Spock swatted the big man. "Dude, don't even put that out there." He turned to Dawson. "What's going on, BD? If we're talking about another Cuban Missile Crisis-type situation, we need to know. I don't want to leave here just to have some other team come in our place."

Dawson turned to Foxglove. "Well? What do you say? Do you want us to cover your six?"

The CIA officer regarded him, his lips pursed, before he gave a curt nod. "This is too important. And having somebody to watch my back increases the likelihood of success." He waved a finger in the air. "But there are too many of you. Pick four, and the rest exfil. We need the Venezuelans to think we all left."

Dawson agreed. A twelve-man team was overkill. They needed to be small, mobile, and as inconspicuous as possible. He turned to Red.

"I want you to take the team to the exfil point and get the hell out of Dodge. Atlas, Spock, Mickey, you're with me."

Niner immediately protested. "Bullshit! You need me! I'm your best shot."

"You were just dead," Dawson reminded him.

"Exactly! And I have arisen, just like the almighty Jesus. Don't you want Jesus on your side?"

Atlas eyed his friend. "Please tell me you don't think you're Jesus."

"I resurrected, didn't I?"

"Buddy, die, then show up for dinner in three days. This little three-minute stint doesn't impress me."

Niner mimicked hurt feelings. "You might not have been impressed, but Angela will be."

"Unfortunately, you can't tell her."

Dawson regarded Niner. He was the Unit's best shot, and his darker skin would blend better than Mickey's. "Are you one-hundred-percent?"

"One-hundred."

"You're sure? No bullshit. You could be putting lives at risk if you're not."

Niner became serious. "BD, I'm good to go. I just got the wind knocked out of me. I'll be all right. You can count on me."

And he could. There wasn't a man on the team who would risk the others just for ego. Dawson's comms squawked, and he held up a finger.

"Zero-One, Control Actual. Come in, over."

"This is Zero-One. Go ahead."

"Permission granted for your team to remain behind in support."

"Copy that, Control. Change of plans. Four of us will be staying for support. The rest will be evacuated. A smaller team is less likely to be discovered."

"Copy that, Zero-One. Permission for a four-man team to remain behind granted. Control Actual, out."

Dawson gave a thumbs-up to the others not privy to the conversation. "We're a go. Now, let's see how we're gonna get from here to there without getting caught."

San Miguel, Venezuela

Herrera drove past the wreckage of yet another SEBIN vehicle and cursed once again. It had to be the Americans. Only they could have pulled this off. There was no way it was a rebel attack. This was going to bite him in the ass. He had been the one who insisted they take the prisoner here rather than to the headquarters in Caracas, where an assault like this would have been impossible. He had been stationed here at the beginning of his career. He was comfortable here, familiar with the area, and it had never occurred to him the Americans would stage a rescue. The fact they had only confirmed his worst fears.

They either knew, or suspected, what was going on west of here.

They reached a clearing ahead, and he stepped out, surveying the area. The distinctive aftermath of a helicopter having landed was evident all around him. They were gone, and any intel passed on by Phoenix to the American corporal was now in Washington's hands.

He stood, hands on his hips, his career crumbling before his eyes. He had hopes, ambitions—but a failure like this? It didn't just end careers, it ended lives.

A burning SUV to his right—left behind by the Americans—sat there, the torching obviously intended to leave no evidence behind beyond the carnage back at the compound.

One of his men jogged over, a radio pressed to his ear. "Sir, we have reports of several helicopters having taken off from here ten minutes ago."

"Are they tracking them?"

"Negative. They're not showing up on radar."

"They won't," muttered Herrera. "They'll stay below radar. Scramble fighters to see if they can intercept them."

"Yes, sir."

The man walked away to relay the orders, but it was useless. By the time they went up and down the chain of command, the Americans would be long gone over international waters, and safe from any retaliation.

He eyed the flaming SUV nearby, his eyes widening as a sudden realization hit him. Spinning around, he searched the area, looking for something that wasn't there. "Where's the second vehicle?"

Everyone stopped what they were doing and began their own searches. One of the men shrugged. "I don't see it. Are we sure there were two?"

"That's what the pursuit team reported," snapped Herrera. "They were chasing two vehicles. Somebody drove that second one out of here. We need to find it. Now!"

He headed back to his ride, his mind racing. Was it just a local contact that had driven it away? He doubted it. They couldn't risk driving a car used in an assault like this. It should have been left with the other one and burned to destroy any evidence. No, something else was going on here. Maybe the Americans didn't have the intel after all. Maybe they didn't know what was going on, only that something was happening.

Maybe his American corporal had remained behind.

And if that were the case, then he might yet save his career. His future. He had to find the American, and this time, when he did, there would be no questions.

He would simply put a bullet in the man's head.

Approaching the Venezuelan Coast

Angus shook his head. "I don't understand why he would choose Niner to stay behind. The dude was dead just a few minutes ago."

Sergeant Eugene "Jagger" Thomas regarded him. "What, you think he should have chosen you?"

Angus gave him a look, fully aware he wasn't the right choice and that Jagger was just teasing him. "Of course not. But do you think Niner's actually good to go?"

Mickey leaned forward, shouting across the hold of the Black Hawk, now thundering toward the coast, hugging the trees below. "Let's put it this way. If you were in Niner's position and you weren't good to go, what would you have done?"

"I would have said so."

"Why?"

"Because I wouldn't want to put anybody in harm's way just because of my ego."

"Exactly. Don't let Niner's joking around fool you. He'd never compromise the mission. If he says he's good to go, he's good to go." Mickey swatted Red on the arm. "Wouldn't be the first time someone's heart stopped around here, would it?"

Red grunted. "Not an experience I recommend."

Angus stared about the cabin. He was new to the team. They were all treating him with respect, treating him as one of the group, and he didn't feel alienated in any way—certainly not intentionally. But these guys had history, history he was only discovering and could never share. The longer he was here, the more of his own he would have—he was new to Delta, and it would just take time.

His assignment to Bravo Team was an incredible honor. Positions on this team usually only opened up if someone died, and in this case, someone had. He wondered if one day he would be considered in the place of someone like Niner, Atlas, or Spock. He doubted it. From what he could tell, those four worked together often, knew what each other was thinking, could anticipate their teammates' moves. They were like a well-oiled machine, and you didn't screw with that. When it worked, you just ran with it. He would find his own group and mesh with them. He would probably never be in the A-Team like the four left behind, but maybe one day he would be on the B-Team instead of relegated to the C-Team.

But that was fine. He had to earn his bones. He didn't care. That was part of it. He wasn't here for personal glory. He was here to serve his country in the best way he knew possible, and that was in Delta, where day in and day out, they fought the battles the American public never heard about.

"We're approaching the mountains!" shouted the pilot from the front.

Red rose to peer ahead as the chopper began climbing, their two Apache escorts flanking them.

A threat alarm sounded.

"We've got a missile lock!" announced the copilot.

Red cursed as he sat back down. "Everybody grab hold of something!"

Angus reached up and grabbed a cargo strap, looping it around his wrist as they continued to climb.

"Deploy countermeasures!" ordered the pilot.

"Deploying countermeasures!" replied the copilot.

Thumping sounds were accompanied by new vibrations in the airframe as they increased altitude. Once they cleared the mountains, the coast was right ahead. They just needed to reach international waters. Five minutes, tops.

But a lot could happen in five minutes.

Angus glanced out a window to see one of their Apache escorts peeling off. He pressed his face to the glass, peering back as the chopper banked slightly. "They're engaging!" he shouted in surprise as missiles streaked from the weapons pods, a wall of lead erupting from the M230 30mm chain gun. "Do they seriously think they can take on fighter jets?"

Mickey leaned forward. "The Venezuelan air force is shit, and their air-to-air is even worse. If you confuse their missile's lock, it can't reacquire."

The Black Hawk abruptly dipped forward and everyone gained a little air. Angus hated to admit it when their lives were at stake, but it was a hell of a lot of fun, reminding him of videos of zero-G training in the vomit comet NASA employed. Now that would be fun. If he had good money, he would pay for a couple of hours on that.

The Black Hawk plunged forward, down the mountainside.

"There she goes, three o'clock!" shouted the copilot.

Angus peered through the window to see a missile streaking above them, detonating harmlessly as its line of sight was lost.

"Coastline ahead!" announced the pilot, and all eyes shifted forward. The skies were clearer compared to when they had inserted, the moonlight glistening off the calm waters. Twelve miles from the coast, and they were clear.

The pilot pushed the engines, rattling the airframe, increasing the throttle beyond the recommended max. Every extra newton of force was critical.

"There's one of our friends," announced Mickey from the other side of the cabin, spotting one of the Apaches.

Angus struggled to see the other, then smiled. "I got his buddy. Looks like they're bugging out," he said as two enemy fighters streaked over the mountain range, both banking to the right.

"No, they're coming in for another run," warned Red. "If this thing's got anything left, you better give her now!" he shouted to the pilot.

"Roger that, Sergeant."

"Where's our air support?"

"Inbound, but they can't do anything within the twelve-mile limit."

"Bullshit! Tell them if they don't engage, we're dead. Add any colorful metaphors you need to get the point across."

"Roger that, Sergeant. Colorful metaphors will be added," the pilot called back with a wry smile as he activated his comms, expletives erupting.

Two missiles launched in the distance.

"Deploy countermeasures!"

"Deploying countermeasures!"

The Black Hawk rattled as chaff detonated, obscuring the airframe. One of the Apaches banked toward the missile, its weapons pods opening up, its own countermeasures deploying. One missile exploded, and Angus pumped his fist, but despite hundreds of rounds, the second missile continued racing forward.

"Brace! Brace! Brace!" shouted the pilot.

Angus cursed to himself. This was it. He was going to die. He should have been a doctor, like his mom wanted. One of the Apaches banked to starboard, and Angus gasped as he realized the pilot wasn't avoiding the incoming missile, but instead putting himself directly in its path.

"Thank you, brothers!" shouted the Black Hawk pilot into his comms as the missile slammed into the Apache, a ball of fire erupting. Angus squeezed his eyes shut, gagging as bile filled his mouth. "Hold on!" cried the pilot, banking hard to starboard. Everyone tumbled. Angus held on to the strap, his entire body in the air as they were peppered with shrapnel from the exploding airframe. The pilot leveled out, alarms sounding in the cockpit. "We're going down!"

Red pushed himself forward. "Can you reach the limit?"

"No damn way!"

"Can you at least reach the water?"

"That I can probably do."

Red smacked him on the shoulder. "Do your best." He turned to the team. "Everybody get ready to bail. Get in the drink, sight the shore, and swim in the opposite damn direction. Understood?"

"Understood!" shouted Angus and the others as a crewman opened the side door. Angus' heart hammered. It was one thing to be under fire, it was an entirely other thing to be in a crashing helicopter.

This was it.

"Hang on!" The pilot pulled up on the stick, killing their speed as the nose came up and the tail dropped.

The crewman peered out and gave a thumbs-up. "Go! Go! Go!"

Mickey went first, the team bailing counterclockwise around the airframe. Angus stepped to the door as the whir of the rotors slowed and the airframe began dropping faster.

"Everybody out!" shouted the pilot. "That means you too," he added, swatting the copilot.

Angus stepped out, plummeting into the dark. His eyes squeezed shut. "Open your damn eyes," he muttered, forcing them open just in time to see the water racing toward him. He hit hard, the shock to his system intense. He sucked in too little air before plunging below the surface. He extended his arms to the sides and spread his legs, killing his downward momentum, then kicked toward the surface, his lungs burning intensely.

Cool air greeted his face as he broke the surface, gasping. He treaded water for a few moments, continuing to gulp in lungsful of air, then he cringed as the helicopter slammed into the water in the distance, an explosion erupting and lighting the entire area. He hadn't been the last of his team out. Red was still in the chopper when he jumped, along with the crew of the Black Hawk itself. How many made it out? Had Red?

He turned to see others stretched out behind him, those who had leaped first already swimming toward his position. He turned, looking ahead, struggling to spot any others, but he didn't see any.

"Red, are you there?" he shouted.

There was no response. He started swimming north toward where Red should be, his eyes peeled for anything in the water. He paused, treading water, then spotted something ahead on the surface, silhouetted by the burning airframe as it slowly sank. He swam as hard as he could, unsure if it was a man or debris he was heading toward.

As he approached, he realized it was absolutely a person—and they weren't flight crew. "Red!" he shouted again. He swam faster, finally reaching the still form. He flipped him over, confirming it was Red, and grabbed the back of his head, lifting it above the water. He smacked Red's cheek. "Red! Are you still with me?"

Nothing.

He punched him in the stomach. Suddenly, Red jerked, water sputtering out, and he coughed and blinked rapidly as he sucked in air.

"You good?"

Red stared up, momentarily disoriented, then finally recognized Angus. "Yeah, yeah, I'm good." He shifted his body weight and began treading water.

Angus backed off slightly. "Thought we lost you there for a minute."

Red reached up and rubbed his head. "Yeah, the chopper began to spin as I was jumping clear. Hit my head on something. Knocked me out cold."

"Good thing it wasn't the blade," laughed Angus, shaking his head. "With that chrome dome of yours, you'd have a hell of a time hiding the scar."

"Or the mortician would," muttered Red, managing a faint snort as the others caught up. "Headcount!"

All eight team members sounded off.

"Did any of the crew make it?" asked Angus.

Mickey shook his head. "Not that I've seen."

"Okay," Red said, scanning the water. "Let's spread out, head north. Hopefully, we'll get lucky and find some of them. If not, we grieve later. Right now, we survive. Remember, we're still within that damn twelve-mile limit."

Phoenix Residence

El Consejo, Venezuela

Valeria sat in the corner, forgotten by the adults rushing in and out. It had been a whirlwind of activity since she had arrived at her uncle's house. Shortly after the phone calls her uncle had made on what she later learned was a satellite phone—untraceable by the authorities—people had begun arriving. Nothing had been said. Instead, the house had been searched using a strange machine brought by one of her neighbors.

Several small devices were found, but they were left alone. Cellphones were placed in front of each of them, playing what sounded like static to her. It wasn't until her neighbor gave a thumbs-up that her uncle finally spoke, though it was still in whispers and from behind closed windows with blinds and curtains shut, preventing anyone from seeing inside. Her uncle obviously feared they were being watched, and the hushed tone suggested they were still concerned about someone listening in.

And those hushed discussions had continued all evening.

The other children were gone. She was the only one there, and they occasionally asked her a question. It was well past her curfew, but her aunt had told her parents where she was so they wouldn't worry—unlike last night, when she had spent the day and night at the embassy with no one knowing what had happened to her. The town had been abuzz with the arrest of her cousin—or so-called cousin. Her family had apparently assumed she, too, had been taken because she had been with him.

Apparently, her uncle's surprise at the news was for the benefit of what the others called bugs.

At least she wasn't the only one in the dark. When her uncle had informed the others that Diego wasn't Diego at all, everyone had expressed shock and demanded an explanation.

"I had to somehow get word to the Americans about what we discovered. If it's what we fear, only they can deal with it. It's far too big for us."

This wasn't the uncle she had grown up with. This was a man everyone in the room treated with reverence, with respect, and kept calling "Phoenix." Why were they calling him that? And why did he have a satellite phone? They were poor. How could they afford something like that?

Her eyes bulged at the first sight of a weapon, and her jaw dropped at the sudden realization of exactly who these people were—who her uncle was. They were rebels. They were the resistance against the Chávez and Maduro regimes. She had heard about them, of course, but it had never occurred to her that there would be any in this area. This was a peaceful farming community. There was nothing of importance here.

Yet here they were, talking, plotting—and her uncle was at the center of it. A shiver raced through her body. It was terrifying. It was exciting. It was like staring in a movie—a spy movie. But in movies, people died. Those were just actors. Here, these were her family, her neighbors, her friends. People she had known all her life. Were they going to die? Was she going to die?

And for what? She thought she had been helping her cousin—helping Diego. But it turned out he was an imposter. A stranger. Someone who had done nothing but lie to her. Anger filled her belly. Everything was a lie. Everything he had said, everything he had told her, everything he had promised her. Now, she might die, her family might die, because of him.

The satellite phone buzzed on the table, and the room fell silent. Her uncle picked it up and answered it. "Hello?…Yes, this is Phoenix…When?…Are you sure?…All of them?…Do you have any idea where they are now?…Understood. Keep me informed."

He ended the call.

"What's going on?" asked one of their neighbors.

"It looks like the Americans just staged a rescue. They got their man out. He was being held at a SEBIN compound in San Miguel."

"Well, that's good news. Hopefully, he'll get word back to Washington—warn them about what we found. What we suspect."

"I never got a chance to tell him what we discovered."

"What do you mean? How the hell didn't you get a chance to tell him?"

Her uncle glared at the challenger. "Because I knew damn well this place was bugged, and the entire town heard my son had returned after fifteen years and descended upon this place, so we barely got a moment alone. I managed to tell him enough that it should get Washington's attention." He tapped the phone. "But our brother tells me that the Americans successfully extracted the rescue team, but five men were left behind, including my so-called son. My friends, he's still here—with help. That tells me he wants to see what we think we found."

"If they're in San Miguel, how in the hell are they going to get here without being caught?"

Her uncle picked up the phone. "I think we need a little family help."

Operations Center 3, CIA Headquarters

Langley, Virginia

Leroux breathed a sigh of relief as the room around him erupted in cheers at the report. Bravo Team and two crewmembers had been recovered and were safely in international waters. Unfortunately, the pilot and copilot had been lost, along with one Apache crew. Four dead. And for what?

They still had no clue what was going on here beyond the rebels thinking something was happening in the jungle, and that a foreign power was involved. What foreign power that was, and what they were doing, were still unknown. Yet he kept going back to October 1962. The Cuban Missile Crisis. The Soviets had sneaked nuclear missiles into Cuba, 90 miles off the Florida coast. It would have meant they could rain death down upon America within minutes. The nation would be defenseless, and it couldn't be allowed.

The world had never been closer to the brink of nuclear war.

Yet cooler heads had prevailed, but not until after 13 long days. The world had survived by the skin of its teeth. Now, here they were, 60 years later, and it might be happening all over again. It might be nothing. It could be a mining operation being set up. Hell, they could be building a resort for the rich. They just didn't know. Just because they saw the offloading of military personnel and equipment didn't mean anything definitive. In Venezuela, the military was involved in everything.

He turned to Tong. "Inform Zero-One on the status of his team."

Tong grinned. "I'm on it."

The doors to the operations center hissed open, and Morrison entered, his eyes on the main display as he joined Leroux at the center of the complex. "I was monitoring. Good work."

Leroux grunted. "Not exactly good."

Morrison's head bobbed. "Yes, we lost four people, but it could have been a lot worse."

"Five, sir."

Morrison's eyebrows rose. "Five?"

"Don't forget we lost our local contact."

"Yes, of course. What's the status of those still in-country?"

"They're trying to head west to get to El Consejo, where the rebels claimed to have spotted the unusual activity."

"How far are they?"

"Two hours' drive—if they could just hit cruise control. But they're going to need to avoid patrols, and if the locals suspect they're there and didn't evacuate with the chopper, they're going to lock down that entire region."

"Any indication of that happening?"

"We're monitoring a lot of encrypted comms traffic from the compound, and satellites are picking up more activity in the area. They're going to be slow to get their shit together at this hour—but they will eventually. Long before our people can make it out on farm roads."

"Understood. Do your best to get them into position."

"Roger that."

"Keep me posted." Morrison headed toward the door, then tossed a departing bombshell over his shoulder at Leroux. "It's time to read your team in. But nothing leaves this room."

"Yes, sir. Thank you, sir."

Morrison left, and Leroux turned to see all eyes on him.

Child spun in his chair. "Well, it's about damn time."

Packman agreed. "Okay, what's really going on, boss?"

"Yeah, something else is definitely going on, because this cover story sucks as bad as an AI-generated novel."

Leroux held up both hands, quieting the peanut gallery. "As I'm sure you've all figured out by now, what you've been told isn't the entire truth." He held up a hand. "And before you get pissed off, just know that I only found out myself a short while ago. Corporal Diego Mendoza is not Corporal Diego Mendoza at all. He's a CIA operations officer codenamed Foxglove. We've worked with him before a couple of times. So, the story is somewhat true. Mendoza's father reached out from Venezuela, but not to his son. Instead, contact was made with the embassy, indicating vital intel serious enough in nature that they believed it could change the strategic balance in the hemisphere. He suggested sending someone in, pretending to be his American son, who is a real person. That entire backstory is true. We just sent someone in Mendoza's place.

"Contact was successfully made. However, minimal information was exchanged. He was arrested before he had a chance to get all the intel. All we do know is that apparently a dock has been built, a road cut into the jungle, and a lot of ships are coming in offloading military personnel and equipment—and that a foreign power might be involved. He wasn't able to find out what foreign power or what the rebels actually suspect is going on. This is why Foxglove and four Bravo Team members remained behind—to gather this intel. Our job is to get them there and get them there safely, because if the rebels are right, and this is serious, we could be facing another crisis like we did sixty years ago."

Packman held up a finger then tilted it toward the screen. "Umm, if we're supposed to make sure they get there safely, maybe we might want to warn them about that."

Outside San Miguel, Venezuela

Fist pumps and high-fives were exchanged at the news the rest of Bravo Team was aboard the USS George Washington. From the sounds of things, it hadn't gone smoothly.

Lives had been lost.

Thankfully, none of Bravo Team had been injured, beyond Red getting a bump on the head, which, according to Tong, he claimed was delivered by the rotor, joking that his hard-headedness had finally paid off and saved his life. His team was safe, but four more lives were to be mourned when this mission was done, a substantial addition to the death toll already tallied for something that could turn out to be much ado about nothing.

They were taking a farmer's access road through fields of crops he couldn't make out in the dark. They were traveling without lights. They couldn't risk being seen. They had to put as much distance as possible between themselves and the SEBIN compound. The town was to the northeast. They were now clear of it, but nothing outran a radio. He had no doubt patrols were being sent out and roadblocks established throughout the entire area. The farther they could get without leaving any footprint, the more likely they were to survive this mission. But all it would take was a single encounter to confirm not only that they were there, but exactly where they were.

Then the Venezuelans would blanket the area with troops, helicopters, and search aircraft. They wouldn't stand a chance.

His comms squawked. "Zero-One, Control. Hold your position immediately, over."

Dawson didn't need to repeat the order, Atlas rapidly bringing them to a halt and killing the engine. "Control, Zero-One. Holding position. Report."

"We have a patrol ahead of you. Two hundred meters."

"Copy that. And evidence they know we're here?"

"Not yet. Stand by."

Dawson quietly opened his door, then winced when the dome light came on. Atlas punched it, shattering the plastic and bulbs, plunging them back into darkness. Dawson gestured for Spock to join him, and the two of them took to the fields, advancing silently toward the road.

A casual conversation could be heard ahead. Dawson held up a fist and they both froze, ears cocked. The conversation was about the previous night, held between several men, filled with nothing but laughter and tall tales.

"Are you done yet?" one of the men asked.

Another voice joined the conversation, barely ten feet from where they were crouching. "Yeah, yeah!"

There was some rustling, then a zipper fastened.

"When you gotta go, you gotta go!"

More laughter followed as whoever had been taking a shit pushed his way through the crops toward the others. An engine roared to life, gears ground, and the patrol was soon on its way.

Dawson rose cautiously, scanning the area, watching them disappear around a bend. He jerked a thumb back toward their ride. "Let's get the hell out of here."

Spock nodded, and they cut over to the farmer's road. "This is going to take forever. Daylight's coming. We need to find a faster way."

Secure Service Entrance Baker, The Pentagon

Arlington, Virginia

Corporal Diego Mendoza scanned the barcode on the pallet, checking it against the manifest on his tablet, then gave a thumbs-up. "That's the last of it."

The delivery driver waved at him. "See you tomorrow night, Diego."

He gave another thumbs-up as his phone vibrated in his pocket. He pulled it out, but didn't recognize the number. He shoved it back in his pocket, letting it go to voicemail as he waved over the forklift driver. The freshly delivered pallets of food needed to be moved into cold storage before they spoiled. The last thing he needed was tainted food to get the brass sick. He wasn't sure if he could be fired for something like that—this was the military, after all—but could he be court-martialed?

He paused. Could he be?

No.

He wasn't sure what punishment he might receive, but he certainly didn't want to find out.

His phone rang again. Once more, it was a number he didn't recognize, and he shoved it back into his pocket. He stepped out of the way as the first pallet was carried past, the second forklift driver already moving into position like a well-oiled machine. It took a lot to feed over 26,000 personnel up to three squares a day.

He was just a corporal, an unimportant cog in the massive organization that was the United States Army, but if the food didn't get delivered and the chow lines dried up, there would be hell to pay. Every single person in this massive facility would be up in arms. Suddenly, everyone would realize how important that one tiny cog with a measly rank of corporal truly was.

A third call vibrated in his pants, and he didn't bother checking it. No messages had yet been left.

Just leave a damn message, and I'll check it when I get a chance. I'm not taking personal calls on duty.

The pallets continued to clear from the loading dock with swift efficiency, and as he marched toward the next phase of the daily operation, it gave him a moment to think of his father. The man was dying, but he was a man he didn't know. It had been 15 years since he had last seen him, and he could barely picture him. He had been too young to have many memories survive. His mother had taken him out of Venezuela after the man's arrest for being a rebel, something his mother assured him wasn't true.

He wanted to visit, to see him before he died. After all, he was his father, but that wasn't possible. Venezuela was the enemy. He was a soldier, and it would never be allowed.

It was unfortunate.

With modern technology, they had managed to exchange the odd text message here and there over the past several years. Mostly birthdays and Christmases, nothing much. They were never close, and after his mother had died years ago, he rarely initiated contact. It had been his aunt who reached out to tell him about the cancer, and he had made a renewed effort to keep in touch and to express his sadness.

But again, this was a man he didn't know. A stranger to him. Yet it was nobody's fault. It wasn't that the man had abandoned them. It was that he had been falsely accused and arrested in a corrupt country. His mother had escaped to give him a better life, and now here he was, an American citizen, serving his adopted country.

And life couldn't be better.

Well, the day shift would be better.

His sergeant walked up. "Any problems with the shipment?"

"No, Sergeant. Complete order today."

"The kitchen will be happy to hear that."

"Yes, Sergeant."

"Carry on."

His phone pulsed, indicating a text message. He waited for the sergeant to turn the corner before pulling it out of his pocket. His eyebrows shot up at the message.

This is Papa. Answer your phone.

Phoenix Residence

El Consejo, Venezuela

Valeria wasn't sure how she felt. She was excited. Angry. Betrayed. And still somehow held a crush. Her uncle had just spoken with her real cousin. She had heard only one side of the conversation, but just knowing that he was real, that he was alive, was exciting. But she was still reminded of the betrayal by the man she thought was her cousin, the man she thought so handsome, so friendly, so charming, so worldly.

She folded her arms, her chin pressed to her chest, deciding anger was the emotion of choice for the moment. "What do we do now?"

"We wait," replied her uncle.

And they did. No one said anything as the night continued to drag on. Almost half an hour had passed before the phone vibrated, and her uncle grabbed it.

"Hello?…Yes, this is Phoenix…Yes, we know about your man, that he was rescued but remained behind with four others." There was a pause, her uncle's head bobbing. "Yes. They're never going to make it here. But we can help…Yes, we know we've been compromised. We've taken precautions…Yes, we're confident we can safely get them in. We'll just need to contact them to coordinate a rendezvous…Very well. I'll await your call."

Her uncle hung up and everyone leaned forward, including herself, eager to hear what had been said.

"That, I'm pretty sure, was the CIA."

Her pulse pounded at the mention of the CIA. It was incredible. Her uncle was so much more than she had ever thought. She couldn't wait to tell her friends, tell them about her trip to Caracas, how it had been at the embassy, that her cousin wasn't actually her cousin.

How her uncle wasn't just a dying man, a dying farmer, but a rebel leader dealing with the CIA.

She frowned. She couldn't tell anyone anything. That was why they were keeping her here—not just because there might be something she could answer if they had a question, but to make sure she told no one what was going on until it didn't matter anymore.

"They confirmed that a four-man team had been left behind with their contact. They're going to coordinate with us. We need to reach out to our brothers in the area. It's critical we find them before the authorities do. Otherwise, they're dead, and our country could be lost forever."

West of San Miguel, Venezuela

Atlas brought them to a halt. If they had traveled ten miles, Dawson would be surprised. They had continued west on back roads, farmers' roads, and things you could barely call roads, guided by the CIA team on the other end of their comms lifeline, satellites far above keeping them safe. But for how much longer. who knew?

Roadblocks had been set up in all directions, patrols intensified, and the occasional helicopter could be heard overhead. They had been lucky so far, but their luck was bound to run out sooner rather than later.

Headlights flashed twice ahead of them, indicating a solution to their problem was perhaps only moments away. Dawson watched through his binoculars as two men stepped out of a delivery truck. One of them waved. Dawson returned the wave out his window.

"Okay, gentlemen. Leave nothing behind. Scrub it down. We don't want any evidence we were driving this thing."

A flurry of activity ensued as every piece of equipment, every bottle of water, and every protein bar were policed. Everyone wiped down their quarter of the car, inside and out. All four doors shut, and they headed toward the delivery truck parked along the side of the road ahead.

"Caracas," said the man.

"Washington."

"Havana."

"Dominican."

The man smiled broadly, extending a hand, the recognition codewords exchanged and accepted. "Good to see you, my friends. Phoenix sends his greetings."

"I look forward to meeting him," said Dawson as he shook the man's hand. "Now let's get out of here. We don't have much time."

They were led to the rear of the truck. The back was thrown open and the second man jumped inside, beckoning them to follow. He snapped on a flashlight, shining it at the floor, showing a false bottom already moved out of the way. "It'll be tight. Normally we don't transport five, but it'll only be for a few hours." He eyed the massive Atlas. "It's going to be *really* tight."

Atlas climbed down into the false bottom. "Story of my life, brother." He stretched out, lying on his side, pressing himself against the edge of the compartment as tightly as he could.

Spock followed but Niner grabbed him. "Hey, if anybody's snuggling against my big man, it's me."

Atlas groaned. "Oh, for crying out loud. Not again."

"I still dream about that, don't you?"

"More like nightmares."

Niner crawled in beside his best friend, then wrapped a leg around him.

Atlas punched him. "Turn around. Back to front."

Niner spun around and squealed in delight as he shoved his ass against Atlas' junk. "Is that an anaconda in your pocket, or are you just happy to see me?"

Atlas stared up at Dawson helplessly. "Please, BD. He was already dead. Nobody will know." He patted his sidearm. "Just one shot could save so much misery."

Dawson snorted as Spock crawled into position. Niner dry-humped him for a moment.

"Is that a Tootsie Roll in your pocket, or are you just happy to see me?"

A rapid high-five was exchanged between Spock and Atlas at Niner's expense.

Their CIA officer glanced at Dawson. "Is it always like this?"

Dawson shrugged. "Actually, everyone's rather well-behaved tonight."

"That's terrifying."

Dawson climbed in, followed by Foxglove. Water bottles were handed to each of them.

"No matter what you hear, you stay quiet. Understood?"

"Understood," replied Dawson as the rest of their gear was stowed at their feet.

The boards were fit into place and cargo stowed at the back was redistributed overhead.

Niner farted.

"Sorry. I've been holding that one in for a while."

Atlas growled. "And you waited until we were in a confined space to finally let it go?"

"Hey, I died. Just remember that."

Spock groaned. "Oh my God. Speaking of death, I think that's what it smells like."

Even Foxglove gagged as Dawson's eyes watered. "My God, Niner. When we get back to base, see a doctor. No healthy human should smell like that."

Their driver smacked a hand against the wall of the truck. "Keep it quiet in there. You're going to get us all killed."

"Understood," replied Dawson.

Everyone fell silent.

Niner launched again.

Operations Center 3, CIA Headquarters
Langley, Virginia

"Don't you find it odd that they haven't moved on Phoenix?"

Leroux turned to find Child spinning in his chair once again, staring up at the ceiling. He had found it odd as well, but hadn't had much time to think about it. Always wanting to encourage the free exchange of ideas among his team, he let Child run with it. "What are you thinking?"

Child dropped his foot, killing his spin, and leaned forward, placing his elbows on his desk. "If they arrested Foxglove, they either knew he wasn't who he said he was, or they knew who the father was. Either way, they know there's a connection. The father wouldn't play along with a man who wasn't his son unless he was indeed Phoenix. They know. They have to know. Or, if they didn't, they had to at least suspect. Phoenix said they were being watched. Remember, Foxglove said they had audio and video surveillance of that house. How the hell did they plant the bug? From what we've been told, that house has been occupied constantly. There's no way some member of the secret police could get inside to plant the bugs. External surveillance? Sure. But keep in mind, this is a small community."

Leroux agreed. "You're right. They'd stand out like a sore thumb. What are you suggesting?"

"I think they've got a traitor in their midst. Somebody's playing the wrong side or both sides. Somebody close to Phoenix."

Child's theory was exactly what Leroux had come up with as well. A thought occurred to him that turned his stomach. He faced Tong. "Any luck finding that dock?"

An exasperated sigh escaped the senior analyst. "I've been able to find *a* dock about ten klicks south of the town. There are good satellite photos taken of the area for years. It's definitely new."

"What's the problem?"

"The problem is, there's no road. It just looks like there's a dock there."

"What about river traffic? Do we have any footage of anything unloading there?"

"No. I've gone back two months. Every time we've got a satellite over the area, there's nothing going on at that dock."

Packman tapped his chin, arms folded. "Could they know our satellite schedule?"

Leroux dismissed the idea. "They don't have that capability."

"According to Phoenix, a foreign power is involved. Maybe *they* have the capability."

Leroux cursed. "The Chinese and Russians would have it. They'd know where our satellites are."

Tong agreed. "Not to mention, they'd probably sell that information if someone like the Iranians or North Koreans wanted it."

"Or the Venezuelans." Leroux stared at the image. "Show me that dock."

Tong brought up the latest image, and Leroux stared at it. "It's not much, is it?"

"Not really. But it doesn't need to be."

Leroux chewed his cheek. There was a dock sitting a few hundred meters up a tributary, and for the life of him, he couldn't see a road. How the hell could you hide a road cut through the jungle? If military personnel and equipment were indeed being offloaded here in great numbers, where were they? There would be some sign of them, some evidence.

His stomach flipped and he bolted to his feet. "This is bait. A setup."

Tong spun in her chair to face him. "Why?"

"They lure us in with bullshit intel, but they don't give us specifics. They're the ones who suggested we send in someone pretending to be Corporal Mendoza. They know we'll send somebody—CIA or some equivalent. They arrest him. We send in a Special Forces unit to rescue him. They capture them and parade them in front of the cameras, claiming America is conducting illegal military operations on their soil. It makes us look bad, and Maduro can use it as an excuse to clamp down even harder. Use it to reinforce his claims that we interfered in the election."

Tong leaned back. "But if they were trying to capture the team sent in to rescue Foxglove, didn't they kind of fail?"

"They definitely failed for that part, but maybe they didn't care if they captured them. Our team left evidence behind. They shot down an Apache over their own territory and a Black Hawk just off the coast, which they can recover if they want. They've got all the proof they need of a military incursion and who committed it. They might already have what they want."

"What do we do? If you're right, they could be heading into a trap. But if you're wrong—"

Leroux sighed. "Then something is still going on in that jungle, and we still need to know." He grabbed his headset. "Get me Zero-One. Secure channel."

Outside El Consejo, Venezuela

The truck they had been in for the better part of the day jerked to a halt, the engine shutting off. Nobody said anything. This wasn't the first time this had happened, and it often meant their escorts were stopping in some public place or at a checkpoint. People could be around.

Two slams of an open palm on the side of the truck suggested things were different this time.

"We're here!"

Sighs of relief escaped all around as the back of the truck was opened. The cargo overhead was repositioned, and the floorboards removed, the light of day pouring in.

"Get me the hell outta here!" demanded Atlas. "I can't take it anymore."

Dawson sat up, extending an arm. Their driver hauled him to his feet. Dawson helped Foxglove—a man he had learned was named Rick, the cramped quarters for hours with the man's junk pressed against his ass resulting in an exchange of first names. Foxglove just sounded like a stripper name, and Dawson had demanded something else to call the man.

Whether it was his real name was irrelevant.

Spock rose then pulled Niner to his feet. Atlas rolled onto his back, and the two of them helped the big man up. Dawson hopped to the ground, surveying their surroundings. They were on a dirt road. A hobbled-together building cut into the jungle stood to the left, the lazy wisps of a fire inside reaching into the canopy overhead.

Gear was retrieved and tossed onto the ground, and Dawson double-checked to make sure nothing had been left behind.

"BD, next time make sure we requisition a cork for this guy's poop chute," rumbled Atlas.

"Hey, it's not my fault I had gas," protested Niner.

"Gas is one thing. What you have is something entirely different."

"Hey, my air biscuits are no worse than yours. It's not like yours smell like roses."

"Shit-covered roses, perhaps," commented Spock. "What the hell did you eat?"

Niner thought for a moment then shrugged. "The only thing I ate different was your"—he swatted Atlas' chest—"girlfriend's food."

"Don't you dare blame her for this."

"Hey, I'm just stating the facts. Something in it gave me gas."

"Something? You know damn well what it was. You're the one who ordered extra cheese, and you're lactose intolerant."

Niner grinned. "Oh yeah. Forgot about that."

"Bullshit! You did it on purpose."

Niner shrugged. "In my defense, I did think we'd be evac'ing on a chopper, not holed up on the floor of a truck for half the damned day."

Spock jerked his chin toward the lone building, and Dawson turned to see a man striding toward them. The man extended a hand. "Welcome, gentlemen."

The English was near perfect. Dawson shook the hand. "Are you Phoenix?"

The man chuckled. "No, and you won't be meeting him. It's too risky. We've discovered he's under surveillance. Please come inside. Though it's rare, this road does sometimes see traffic."

Gear was grabbed, and they all headed toward the building. Dawson's comms squawked in his ear.

"Zero-One, Control Actual. Come in, over."

Dawson held back, activating his comms. "This is Zero-One. Go ahead, Control."

"Zero-One, exercise extreme caution. We believe there's a possibility this is all a setup."

Rojas Residence

El Consejo, Venezuela

Valeria stretched, shoving her left arm above her head, her right leg extending toward the foot of her bed. She switched sides, repeating the process, then rolled over, squeezing her eyes shut. She stifled a yawn. It took her a moment to realize she was in her bedroom, and another moment to remember how she got here. It had been late in the night when her father collected her. She had stumbled home, nothing going on anymore that was of interest. She had actually fallen asleep in the corner, and when her father had woken her, even her uncle had gone to bed.

But now the sun poured through the window. The roosters' morning call was long gone, and she glanced at her alarm clock, surprised to discover it was afternoon. She quickly dressed and was about to open her bedroom door when she heard a voice. She paused, pressing her ear to the door. It was her father. She couldn't make out what was being said, and it was only his voice with long pauses.

He was on the phone.

My phone!

She retrieved it off the nightstand, unplugging the charger, and frowned. It was down to less than 20%. Had it charged at all overnight? She flipped the light on and off, finding it dead. The power was out again.

What else was new?

She checked her phone, confirming what she already knew. No signal. When the power went out here, so did the cellphone towers. There were no generators to provide backup power in a town like this. Maybe in Caracas they had them, but not here. They were lucky to have any coverage whatsoever.

But if the power was out, then how was her father on the phone?

Her heart hammered as last night's intrigue flooded back. Everything now seemed suspicious. She opened her door a crack, wincing at the loud creak. She froze, but the conversation continued. She pressed her ear to the sliver of an opening, finally making out what her father was saying.

"No, I don't think there's any chance of that. Not now…If I'm caught, they'll kill me…Threaten my daughter again, and I'll kill you…Fine, I'll see what I can do. But Phoenix is your problem. You deal with him…Threaten me again, and I'll kill you…No, Phoenix is your problem. Deal with him yourself. I'm done with it. It's too dangerous…Fine, throw me in prison, but I'm done. Touch my…If I see you again, I'm going to slit your throat…Fine, I'll try to plant one the next time I'm there. Then I'm out. I don't care what you do or say."

Her father cursed, and footfalls approached, the conversation evidently over. She stepped back from the door and sat on the edge of her bed, staring at her phone as her heart pounded. "Papa, is the power out again?" she asked, her voice quavering slightly.

"Yes, it is," her father called from the hallway as he passed her door. "Thank Caracas for their top-notch management."

Thankfully, he didn't enter her room. She sat there trembling. Her father was a traitor. He was working for the government. Working against her uncle.

What the hell am I supposed to do?

Outside El Consejo, Venezuela

"Did they say why they thought it might be a setup?" asked Spock as the five of them huddled in a corner of the ramshackle home.

Dawson shook his head. "No. It's just a suspicion based upon the fact they haven't found the road that was referred to, and that Phoenix hasn't been picked up yet."

"Yeah, that doesn't sound right to me either." Niner, sitting in the only chair at Dawson's insistence, frowned at the view in front of him. "Can I please stand up? As much as you think this might be a view I'd enjoy, all I'm seeing is crotch and ass."

Spock snorted. "Be thankful this is temporary and you're not in a wheelchair."

"And be thankful you're not dead," rumbled Atlas. "All you'd be seeing is dirt."

Niner looked up at his friend. "I'm not sure that's how the afterlife works."

"In all seriousness," said Spock, "what should we do?"

Dawson folded his arms and leaned against the wall. It creaked. "We keep our eyes open. If this is a setup and we can't get out, we surrender and let the diplomats handle things."

Rick cleared his throat, speaking for the first time since the revelation. "Maybe you should abort. I'll stay here. You guys arrange an extraction. One person draws a hell of a lot less attention than five."

Dawson dismissed the idea. "No. You'd stand no chance if they found you."

Rick smirked. "You might be surprised."

"Uh-oh, we've got another Kane here," interrupted Spock.

Rick laughed. "I've worked with him, and I'm afraid to say I'm nowhere near as good as that man's ego thinks he is."

Spock cocked an eyebrow. "If you were, I don't think we'd be having this conversation."

"Why? You think he's that much better than me?"

"No. It's that that man's confidence seems to make him bulletproof."

Dawson held up a hand, cutting off the conversation. "We're going to stick together for now. I'm not aborting this mission just because of a suspicion from Langley."

"What about the fact they haven't been able to find this road?" Atlas turned to Rick. "What do you think?"

"I don't know. Maybe they found the wrong dock. Maybe they've disguised the road somehow. But there's only one way to find out."

Dawson agreed. "We need to put eyes on that dock."

West of San Miguel, Venezuela

Herrera slowly paced around the abandoned truck. Bullet holes peppered the vehicle, leaving no doubt this was the missing transport that had carried the American assault team from the complex. He gestured at the mud. "There are at least three or four, maybe even five, sets of footprints here. Our corporal isn't alone anymore."

One of his men radioed the new information to the search teams as Herrera continued to circle the scene. Another soldier, searching the vehicle, reemerged. "Sorry, Colonel, there's nothing here. I get the distinct impression they wiped it down. We're probably not going to find anything."

Herrera said nothing. It was exactly as he had expected. Back at the extraction point, the other ride had been torched to destroy any evidence. Everyone within miles had heard the helicopter land in the dead of night, so it made no difference. But here, in the middle of nowhere, a fire blazing would have revealed their position.

He stepped over to the driver's side and opened the door, finding the keys in the ignition. Why had they abandoned the vehicle? He sat and pressed down on the clutch and brake, then turned the key. The engine roared to life. He revved it a couple of times, the clutch still engaged, and the engine sounded fine. He switched it off.

"They're either on foot, or they met someone and switched vehicles." He climbed out and followed the footprints, finding them converging near a set of tire treads that clearly belonged to a truck. He cursed. "They were picked up by a truck." He indicated another fresh set of footprints that came from the driver's side and passenger side. "Have them looking for some sort of transport. Two in the cab. Our Americans are in the back, perhaps under floorboards."

He cursed again. It had to be dissidents, and if they were involved, the Americans could be anywhere now. He pursed his lips as he stared off into the distance. Not anywhere. They stayed behind for a reason, and there was only one reason he could think of.

He spun on his heel. "We need to get back to El Consejo immediately."

South of El Consejo, Venezuela

Dawson crouched in the brush along the side of the river with Rick. Spock was half a klick north, watching for any approaching vessels, while Atlas and Niner covered their sixes, just in case anyone paid them a visit from the road they had used to get here. It was evening now, and so far, there was no sign of betrayal.

Their local contact had taken them to the dock in question. From what he could see through his night vision gear, it was definitely newly constructed. Its surface was reinforced to handle heavy equipment, but more importantly, there was definitely a road leading into the jungle. Why Langley couldn't see it, he wasn't sure.

He zoomed in, carefully scanning left to right. There was no one in sight.

"Zero-One, Control. Come in, over."

"This is Zero-One. Go ahead, Control."

"Zero-One, be advised, the satellite is below the horizon. We now have no coverage of your position, over."

"Acknowledged, Control." He glanced over at Rick. "Well, if anything is going on here and it's tied to our satellites, we might be about to find out just how well-informed they are."

Rick grunted as he peered through his own set of binoculars. "Have you noticed the canopy?"

Dawson pressed his glasses to his eyes, peering across the river once again. "What do you mean?"

"You can see the road, but look above the road. What aren't you seeing?"

Dawson stared, missing it at first, and was about to say so when he cursed. "No stars."

"Exactly. The canopy's intact. They cut the road but somehow managed to keep the branches overhead in place."

"How the hell did they manage that?"

Rick sat back. "I don't know, but we need to get a better look. That road is wide enough to take transport trucks. I could see maybe preserving some of the canopy at the beginning of the road, just to disguise it from the river. But all the way to its destination?" He regarded Dawson. "You don't think Langley missed it, do you?"

Dawson dismissed the notion. "No way. These guys are the best. I've worked with them in the past quite a bit. There's no way they'd miss something like that."

"Agreed. I've worked with them too. They're good, and I recognize the voice of Control Actual. He's one of the best they've got, if not the best."

Spock's voice crackled over the comms. "Zero-One, Zero-Five. I've got activity. Looks like at least a two-hundred-footer coming your way, over."

"Copy that, Zero-Five. Try to get some footage and upload it to Langley. Let's see if we can identify the vessel, over."

"Roger that. Zero-Five, out."

Dawson cocked his ear and could hear the boat's engine in the distance. This could be the moment of truth. Was there something going on in the jungle? Was there something that could indeed change the strategic balance in the hemisphere?

"There it is," said Rick, pointing to their left.

The nose of the boat appeared around the bend, heading into the tributary they were now positioned in.

"They're running dark," observed Dawson as he peered through his binoculars. The night vision gave him an eerie glow, revealing what, for all intents and purposes, appeared to be a ghost ship. He spotted movement on the front deck—crew preparing to dock.

"We've got activity at the dock," reported Rick.

Dawson quickly checked to see personnel emerging from the jungle, a light now visible perhaps 100 yards from shore. He returned his attention to the approaching ship, still running dark. There was a flare as someone lit a cigarette directly in his line of sight. Dawson cocked an eyebrow at Rick. "Now he's definitely not Venezuelan." He activated his comms. "Control, Zero-One. Please tell me you got that, over."

Langley, jacked into the feed from his binoculars, responded a moment later. "Affirmative, Zero-One. Running the face now."

"What did you see?" asked Rick.

"Let's just say they definitely didn't look Russian."

Phoenix Residence

El Consejo, Venezuela

Valeria sat in the corner of her uncle's living room once again, saying nothing, uncertain as to what to do. Her father was a traitor. She was certain of it. No, not certain. Perhaps she was confused. Wasn't her uncle the actual traitor? Didn't one have to be a traitor to their country? That was certainly one definition. Her uncle might be a traitor to his country, though as she thought about it, he was more a traitor to the regime that controlled the country, rather than the country itself. Didn't rebels love their country? And if her father was pretending to be a supporter of the rebel cause, then he was indeed a traitor to that cause.

But who was on the right side?

In school, she was taught the regime was on the right side of everything. It was drummed into them day in and day out. But when she returned home at the end of the day, she would always be set straight by her mother, even her father, and certainly many of her other relatives and neighbors.

Nobody here seemed to support the regime.

And she couldn't understand why her father would.

Perhaps they had threatened him. Perhaps they had told him if he didn't cooperate, they would harm her or her mother. It did fit with the conversation she had overheard. Whoever was on the other end of that call had certainly threatened them all.

But what was she supposed to do? If she told her uncle what she knew, what would they do to her father?

But if she didn't?

She bit down on her knuckle hard, the pain bringing her focus back, settling the trembling that threatened to expose her. Hardly anyone had been here all day. The flurry of activity from last night was over, though her uncle continued to take whispered phone calls as the windows remained covered.

She had been the only visitor for hours, besides her father. She had watched him like a hawk to see if he planted a bug, but she hadn't spotted anything. She wondered if perhaps he had decided to ignore his orders. More likely, he just hadn't found the opportunity, because her uncle, too, had been watching. If something new was found, with so few visitors, they might realize who the guilty party was. Then what would happen to her father? Torture and death at the hands of the secret police? Or torture and death at the hands of the rebels—her own friends and neighbors?

She wasn't sure what she would prefer. She had to think the secret police would be better at it, would cause more pain, and would show no mercy. But to be tortured by people you had known your entire life?

She shuddered. She couldn't imagine it.

"What's wrong, little one?"

She flinched. Her uncle was staring at her from his chair. "Nothing," she stammered. "I'm all right."

"You should go home. You shouldn't be here."

"But I want to be."

He smiled at her. "It's exciting, isn't it? Being privy to something that no one else is?"

She nodded furiously in agreement. "Absolutely. Scared and excited at the same time."

"You've done your part," he said. "You helped by getting us word about what happened. You probably saved lives."

"Is that what you're trying to do?"

"Yes."

"But aren't you a traitor?"

Her uncle chuckled. "I suppose that depends on whose side you're looking at things from. From the government's perspective, yes, I'm a traitor. From my country's perspective, no. I love my country, but I hate what it's become. The regime that's ruled us for so long, that's ruined our nation—once proud, once rich—it must be removed so that democracy can be restored, so that we can once again rejoin the rules-based order. When your allies are Russia, China, Cuba, North Korea, Iran—you know you're on the wrong side of things."

She had heard of all those countries, of course, though she knew little about them. "Are they bad?"

"Oh, they're definitely bad. The worst of the worst. If just Russia, China, Iran, and North Korea were removed from the face of the Earth, we might just achieve world peace."

"Wouldn't that mean the death of a whole lot of people?"

"Yes, it would, which is why it's not a realistic nor moral dream. Remove their governments, give the people power, perhaps the same can be achieved. None of these bad countries are bad because their people are bad, but because their governments are. Like the secret police—they're the worst of the worst."

She stared at her feet. "What if…" She hesitated, uncertain as to what to say. "What if someone is forced to do something they don't want to do? Like by the secret police. Are they a traitor?"

Her uncle regarded her. "I would say they're a victim."

"A victim?" It was an interesting word. Was her father a victim? Perhaps he wasn't a traitor after all. They wouldn't hurt a victim, would they? She squeezed her eyes shut, holding back the tears that demanded release.

"What's wrong, my child?"

She couldn't hold it any longer, and she choked out what she had come here to say all those hours ago. "I think my father's a victim."

Operations Center 3, CIA Headquarters

Langley, Virginia

"I don't know. Certainly looks Chinese to me," said Child, staring at the display, an isolated frame from Dawson's binoculars being mapped, facial recognition points illuminated.

Leroux had to agree. From the accompanying video, it appeared the man was tall, and from his experience, that was rare among the North Koreans. But they couldn't jump to conclusions—not yet, despite speculation being part of his business.

With the points mapped, the computer began its search. Leroux glanced over at Tong, staring intently at her station, running the face through every database they had. If the subject was a peon, they might not have him. But if he was a somebody, there was a chance they might just identify him.

And he had to be a somebody. He was there, in the middle of the Venezuelan jungle, on a boat traveling without lights in the dark, docking at a newly constructed dock. For a Venezuelan, that alone would be odd, but for this man?

He was definitely somebody.

And who that somebody was might have just been narrowed down by the flurry of immediate activity after the satellite went below the horizon. That was damn good intel, and the Venezuelans didn't have the capability for that level of precision.

But the Chinese certainly did.

Morrison entered the operations center, and Leroux rose, having informed his boss the moment they had spotted the face. "Anything yet?" asked Morrison as he joined him.

"Not yet. We're running the face now."

Morrison folded his arms, staring at the image. "Certainly looks Chinese."

"That's what I said," said Child.

Morrison glanced over his shoulder at the youngest team member. "But as I'm sure you know, we can't jump to conclusions."

"Of course, sir," Child murmured, burying his head behind his station. Morrison and Leroux exchanged smirks.

"He's definitely Chinese," pronounced Tong, tapping away at her keyboard and turning her attention to the main display. "His name is Colonel Chen Tao of the People's Liberation Army." She whistled. "Okay, this can't be good."

"What?" asked Morrison and Leroux at the same time.

"Kane identified him last year. According to what we've got on him, he's associated with their hypersonic missile program."

Leroux tensed, a knot forming in his stomach. "Wait a minute. Do we know if he's still involved with that program?"

"There's nothing here indicating he isn't. But we're lucky to have anything on him at all."

"Contact Kane. Have him poke around, see if we can find out more about this guy," ordered Morrison.

"On it."

Morrison turned to Leroux. "If they're putting hypersonic missiles into Venezuela…"

"But what would be the point? It's not really a deterrent. It's not like they'd ever launch against us. It would be suicide."

"The Soviets weren't going to launch their missiles against us either," Morrison pointed out. "But it was a deterrent against us launching against them. By putting missiles in Cuba, it meant that if we launched, they could hit us long before our missiles reached their targets. It changed the equation. At the time, if we wanted to do a strategic launch—whether minimal or full assault—they could take out our capacity to respond after our first launch. But you're right. This"—he waved his arm at the screen—"makes no sense. Putting conventional hypersonic missiles into Venezuela? What does that accomplish?" He tapped his chin. "What's the range?"

Tong pulled up the specs, throwing them on the main screen. "If we assume they're putting in their latest and greatest, they could pretty much cover the entire continental US. Certainly the entire eastern seaboard and southern United States."

Morrison headed for the door. "I need to talk to Washington." He stabbed a finger at the display. "Find out if they've already deployed those missiles. Because if they have, this could mean war."

South of El Consejo, Venezuela

Dawson continued peering through his binoculars at the flurry of activity across the river. The moment the loading ramp at the back of the ship dropped, forklifts and transport trucks—hidden away in the forest— emerged, their lights blazing. The Venezuelans were clearly confident no one was watching. Pallet upon pallet of material was loaded into the trucks, which then headed into the jungle.

"See that?" asked Rick.

"What?"

"Check that load coming off now."

Dawson turned his attention to a set of large black crates now being offloaded. "Our Chinese fish out of water definitely seems to be concerned with these ones. I'm counting six so far."

"So far, but here's two more now. What do you think's in those?"

"I don't know, but I'm guessing they're what this is all about."

"I think you're right." Rick stripped out of his gear, then plunged into the water.

Dawson cursed but didn't call after him. They couldn't risk giving away their position. The impetuous action reminded him of working with Kane or Jack or any other CIA officer—they were used to acting alone, making split-second decisions, and rarely asking permission. They all lived by the old adage that it was better to ask for forgiveness than permission.

He didn't bother watching the CIA officer swim across the river. Instead, he continued to scan the shore, just in case somebody spotted the fool. Rick reached the riverbank just downstream and disappeared into the jungle.

"What the hell is he up to?" Dawson muttered, tilting his head slightly, cocking an ear as he continued to monitor. There was no sign the man had been spotted, and Dawson prayed it stayed that way.

The Venezuelans had to know by now that some of the team had remained behind. Going on foot hadn't been an option, so they had to use one of the two rides at their disposal. Dawson was quite certain the secret police could count past one—they would have noticed the missing vehicle. It was only a matter of time before they found it, if they hadn't already.

They would know at least one person had stayed behind. And if they weren't absolute fools, they would have spotted the footprints in the damp dirt that led to tire treads. From there, it wouldn't take much to determine a transport truck had been involved.

The Venezuelans were definitely searching for them. The question was, how far behind were they? They had to know this was the destination. For some reason, though, they hadn't blanketed the area with troops. Likely, they didn't want to confirm anything important was going on here by drawing attention to the area. With the satellite out of position and the next one not coming into range for another 25 minutes, this would be the time to hit the area with everything they had.

The idea left Dawson uneasy.

He activated his comms. "Bravo Team, this is Zero-One. Keep an eye out. Something doesn't feel right. If you encounter the enemy, fall back to the river, do not engage, over."

A string of acknowledgments came in, though, as expected, there was nothing from Rick. He would be running under radio silence. Dawson continued to peer across the river. The activity was slowing, the cargo unloading apparently finished. The ramp was raised, lines were cast, and the ship slowly pulled away from the dock, heading back up the tributary.

"Zero-One, Zero-Five. She's continuing south down the main river. Looks like she's picking up speed, trying to make up for the lost time she was docked, over."

"Copy that, Zero-Five. Join me at my position, over."

"Roger that. Zero-Five, out."

Dawson's Spidey sense was tingling. He flinched at a sound to his right and spun around, his weapon aimed directly at Rick's head as it emerged from the water. Dawson lowered the weapon. "What the hell was that all about?"

Rick grinned. "Planting a little tracker."

"I wasn't aware we had any."

Rick jerked his chin toward Dawson's comms. "Poor-man's tracker. I put mine on the truck with those fancy crates. Now all we gotta do is sit back and see where they go."

"Just that easy, huh?"

"Yep."

Dawson frowned. "Something tells me you better pray they don't find it or they're gonna know we're here."

Phoenix Residence

El Consejo, Venezuela

Valeria sat in the corner, her uncle continuing to search the living room as he peppered her with questions about what she had overheard. He made her repeat it over and over, picking away at the details.

Her stomach protested.

"I think I'm going to be sick," she muttered.

Her aunt rushed her to the bathroom, and Valeria hugged the bowl, throwing up. This had to be how it felt to be a traitor. She had betrayed her father. He was guilty, yes, but she had no idea what his motivations were, what his reasons were. They could be blackmailing him into doing what he was doing. He could have just been protecting her and her mother from harm.

And she had given him up.

And her uncle was irate.

She flushed the toilet.

"Rinse out your mouth," instructed her aunt, her voice gentle, sympathetic.

A curse erupted from the living room as Valeria swished water in her mouth and spat it into the sink. She turned on the tap, waving her hand in front of the stream of water to make sure she washed the remnants down the drain. Her aunt gave her a hug and they headed back to the living room to find her uncle holding a small device triumphantly in the air.

He dropped it on the floor then stomped on it with the heel of his shoe.

"Where did you find it?" asked her aunt.

He kicked the couch. "Tucked between the cushions. Right where he was sitting."

Valeria's shoulders shook at the confirmation. Her father was who she thought—a traitor working for the secret police. "I'm so sorry, Uncle," she whispered.

He glared at her, his expression stern. Then his face abruptly relaxed, and he held out an arm. "Come here, child."

She reluctantly shuffled forward, and he wrapped an arm around her.

"This isn't your fault. I'm not mad at you. You did the right thing by telling me."

"What are you going to do to my father?"

"Nothing."

Her eyes shot wide with a renewed sense of hope. "Nothing?"

"Well, not exactly nothing."

"What do you mean?"

"Now that we know who he works for, we'll use him."

"How?"

"It's called misinformation." He stared down at the crushed bug on the floor. "I probably shouldn't have done that," he muttered. He picked up the satellite phone and made a call. "This is Phoenix. We've been compromised. Juan Rojas is a traitor."

He ended the call as a roaring engine approached. He headed for the window and moved the curtain slightly aside, cursing. Valeria recoiled in fear as red and blue lights flashed outside, visible through the thin curtains in the late evening darkness.

"Where are they going?" asked her aunt, her voice hushed, the fear obvious.

Her uncle cursed yet again as he turned and stared at Valeria. "They're going to your family's house. We have to get you out of here. Now."

Outside the Rohas Residence

El Consejo, Venezuela

Herrera stepped out of the car as his men surrounded the house, four of them breaching the main entrance. He had arrived several hours ago and been briefed on the latest surveillance of the rebel cell believed to be operated by a man named Phoenix, whom they suspected lived in this sleepy farming community. As soon as the newly planted bug had gone offline, it was clear their asset had been compromised before it had been discovered and destroyed.

The girl had betrayed her own father.

It was impressive. And it meant he had been right. She might not be a threat today, but what she had done—giving up her own family for the cause—proved she could be a threat tomorrow.

He wouldn't do anything to her just yet, beyond using her as leverage.

The girl's father was hauled outside by two of his men for all the neighbors to see, many poking their heads out of doors and windows, curious as to what was going on. None would dare challenge him today.

He had a sense he was in the heart of rebel territory. There was a reason Phoenix was here, even if they still had no proof. The bugs already installed weren't picking up anything, though the fact the newly planted one had been working before it was destroyed suggested the bugs that Rojas had surreptitiously hidden over recent weeks had been discovered or overridden somehow. Nothing but static had been picked up on them since yesterday. With everything going on, that was simply too much of a coincidence.

The girl's father was shoved into the back of a car and Herrera opened the door, peering inside. "We meet again. Now, tell me where they are."

The man's eyes narrowed. "Who?"

"The Americans, you fool! Where are they?"

"I have no clue."

Herrera reached out and grabbed the man by the throat, squeezing hard. "If you don't know, then who does?"

"I...I don't know."

He tightened his grip as Rojas struggled for breath. "Then perhaps your daughter knows."

"No, don't touch her!"

"Then tell me something I want to hear. Otherwise, she becomes a plaything for the boys."

Operations Center 3, CIA Headquarters

Langley, Virginia

Leroux stared at the display, shaking his head. "This is getting frustrating."

"Tell me about it," agreed Tong as they watched a red dot slowly move deeper into the jungle, away from the dock. Foxglove's cleverly planted comms continued to transmit its location, and there was no indication the Venezuelans had detected it. And why would they? It would never occur to them to look for it.

But what was frustrating was that there was still nothing showing up on the satellite. There was clearly a road there. They had pulled up daytime shots of the route the convoy was taking, and there was still nothing visible. Just jungle. No road.

Leroux's arm darted out, and he pointed at the screen, his hand held vertically. "We know the route they're taking, but there's no damn road. Yet there has to be. There's no way you can go through a jungle like that without bobbing and weaving around the tree trunks. They have to have cut a path. So, what's going on?"

"They must have some sort of cover," suggested Child.

Leroux's head bobbed. "Wait a minute. We can't see a road. But that's to the naked eye. Do we have any thermal imaging of that area?"

"Negative," said Tong. "It's a low-priority area."

"What's the nearest satellite that could give us thermals?"

Tong worked her station. "Defense SAT Charlie-Charlie-Four-Two."

Leroux headed for the door. "We're going to need to get that re-tasked. We need better eyes on that area. But one thing's clear."

"What?" asked Tong, as Leroux reached the door.

"You don't go to that much trouble to hide a road if there's just an amusement park at the end of it."

"Pick up the daughter and take her to my quarters. I'll be there shortly," Herrera said, ending the call. He stared at his prisoner. "What's your daughter's name?"

"Valeria," stammered the man.

"Valeria," repeated Herrera. "I always like to know their names before I spend the night with them."

His prisoner's eyes bulged. "You wouldn't dare! She's just a girl. Just a child!"

"Innocence. It's such an attractive quality, don't you agree?"

"You're disgusting! How can you even think such a thing?"

"I wouldn't have to if you cooperated. Now, you got us out here— finish what you started. Waste any more of my time, and I'm going to introduce your daughter to the joys of being a woman."

Tears flowed down the prisoner's face. He was broken. This ploy worked almost every time. Herrera had no intention of touching the child, and he would shoot any man who would. He wasn't a pig. He wasn't a monster. He was a patriot. He had called his voicemail, faking the order, the command to pick up the girl never given. But it would be if her father refused to cooperate.

The man was associated with a dissident group, but they had quickly determined he was a nobody—a hanger-on, somebody looking to feel important. He wasn't smart enough to truly be anything significant. But his daughter? She was beautiful. At the right age to believably be an object of desire. Experience had taught him that this tactic left fathers vulnerable almost every time.

The suspected group had been placed under increased surveillance due to the activities south of here, and further increased when the visa for Mendoza had been issued. As soon as they got wind the Americans were involved, their plan had been altered. Rojas had been coerced into planting the bugs.

The man was a traitor—a traitor to his cause, a traitor to his country. All these people were. They were the reason Venezuela was in such trouble. It wasn't mismanagement by the regime. No, it was the lies spread by those who didn't support the direction their leaders wanted to take them. Because of the lies they spread, the international community treated the country like a pariah. They imposed sanctions, imposed suffering. Life was difficult enough already. Sanctions raised prices, caused industries to fail.

Why couldn't Venezuela produce oil like they used to? Because they couldn't get the spare parts to repair the equipment. And that was because of sanctions. That was because of countries like America. All because they believed the lies. It was his job to root out those responsible, to find those who would destroy their country through greed, through disinformation.

The government had come to an arrangement with the Chinese, one that would ensure their security, one that would ensure their economy, and by extension, their people, could thrive. And there was no way in hell he was letting the Americans interfere with that.

They were only days away from implementing the plan, and once it was in place, it would be too late. Once the deterrent was set up, Venezuela wouldn't just be the most powerful nation in South America—it would be untouchable by the Americans.

He waggled his phone at the still-silent prisoner. "Well? What's it going to be? Your daughter's virtue, or the location of some traitors to their country?"

Rojas' shoulders slumped, his head falling forward. "Keep driving east. Maybe five kilometers. There's an access road on the left. Take it. Not far in, there's a house on the left. That's where they are."

Herrera smiled. "Now, was that so hard?" He gestured to the driver, and they started forward, the others following behind with their red and blue lights now dimmed. He checked his watch. They were within the satellite coverage gap of the dock. If all had gone to plan, the latest shipment had already arrived and been unloaded. If something had gone wrong, he would have heard by now.

It meant the Americans might not yet know what was going on.

They continued to drive in silence until his prisoner pointed ahead. "Take a left here."

The driver slowed, making the turn down a barely visible road. He hit the brakes, cutting their speed dramatically as they bounced violently. "Sorry, Colonel. To call this thing a road—" He was cut off as they got caught in another rut, jarring everyone. Herrera, not wearing his seatbelt, pressed a hand against the roof for balance. "I see something."

Herrera leaned forward, spotting a structure. "Is that it?"

Rojas nodded. "Yes."

"How many people?"

"I have no idea. I only know the location. I'm sorry."

"Kill the lights."

The driver complied, and the others behind them followed suit.

"This is far enough." They came to a halt and he stepped out, the other vehicles emptying as well, his team gathering around him. "They're inside. Unknown numbers. Remember, I want them alive. Especially the Americans."

"Yes, Colonel," echoed the team leads.

The building was quickly surrounded, the door kicked in, followed by shouts and the crash of furniture. After a couple of minutes, an all-clear came in over the radio. Herrera approached the hovel and stepped through the door to find a lone man with a gray beard sitting in a chair, half a dozen guns aimed at him.

"Is this it?" asked Herrera, barely masking his surprise and disappointment.

"Yes, sir. We searched the place. He's the only one here."

Herrera drew his weapon and pressed it against the man's forehead. "Where are the Americans?"

Operations Center 3, CIA Headquarters

Langley, Virginia

"Is the satellite in position yet?" asked Leroux. The re-tasking had been approved by Morrison, who agreed they needed unexpected eyes on the target area—eyes with more capability than what they currently had.

"Coming into position now," replied Tong.

The United States had a vast array of satellites overhead, observing the world. These assets monitored Russia, China, North Korea, Iran, and others. Knowing they were being watched helped keep things in check. It certainly made things inconvenient, increasing costs. If you could only operate within certain narrow windows, if you constantly had to hide what you were doing, it wasted time and money.

And the more the enemy wasted those precious resources, the more likely they were to lose the game, just like the Soviet Union. With the faked Strategic Defense Initiative tests, the Soviets had been terrified that America was about to launch lasers into space that could shoot their missiles out of the sky and start forest fires. It had all been bullshit, but it had forced the Kremlin to spend billions upon billions they didn't have, eventually bankrupting themselves, leading to the loss of the Cold War and the dissolution of America's greatest enemy.

Unfortunately, the Russian people had turned out to be morons and elected a strongman leader, becoming a threat once again. But Russia wasn't really the threat anymore. Their military had been decimated by the war in Ukraine. China—that was the real threat. But even China didn't know everything America had in the sky. Satellites with stealth technology, rendering detection nearly impossible with paneling that absorbed rather than reflected light, leaving them barely visible to the naked eye from space, let alone from the ground, could be positioned wherever needed.

And one of those satellites was moving into position now, with sensors that might finally give them the answers they had been looking for. Where the hell was the road, and why couldn't they see it?

"Visuals coming in now," said Tong, jerking her chin toward the main display.

Leroux looked up to see a shot of their target location, still at an angle, as the satellite moved into position directly overhead. It had geostationary capabilities and would sit over the target for as long as the approvals lasted. Right now, he couldn't think of anything more important going on in the world than what they were doing. If there was a chance the Chinese were setting up a base in the jungles of Venezuela, with hypersonic missiles capable of targeting almost the entire United States within minutes, this was currently the greatest threat the country faced.

"There's the dock," said Packman, leaning forward.

"Looks like that boat's gone," added Child.

"We already knew that."

Child gave Packman the side-eye. "Did I sound surprised?"

It wasn't news. They had witnessed the unloading of the ship and its rushed departure through the feed on the ground provided by Bravo Team.

"Satellite is in position," reported Tong.

Leroux rose, peering at the crystal-clear image of the dock and its immediate surroundings.

"I still don't see the road."

"It has to be there." He gestured at another display showing everything they were tracking, including the truck with Foxglove's comms, still moving away from the river. He tapped his chin. "We know it's there. It has to be covered somehow. Something like that would require damn good netting, designed specifically to match its surroundings. Otherwise, it would stick out like a sore thumb." He snapped his fingers. "Let's see the thermals. If it is netting, it should absorb heat differently than the trees."

"Stand by." Tong tapped at her station, and the display switched.

Leroux smiled at the bright red trail leading directly through the jungle. "There's our road."

Child whistled, spinning in his chair. "Hello, highway to hell."

Leroux's smile disappeared as he spotted something to the west. "Show me Bravo Team's position," he snapped.

Tong, sensing the urgency, furiously executed the orders. The image shifted, showing five souls clustered together along the shoreline—and at least a dozen in the trees, closing in on their position.

South of El Consejo, Venezuela

Dawson checked his watch. The additional satellite coverage should be in position by now and answers would hopefully be forthcoming.

"Do you think they'll find the road?" asked Spock, having rejoined them now that they had indeed determined this was the correct dock in question.

"If it's there, they'll find it. Even if they don't, we know it's there. They've tracked those comms for several miles now."

Rick nodded. "And they've been heading in a pretty straight line, apparently. There's a road there. We just need to find out where it goes."

"And how far it goes. If it's a few klicks, we can do that on foot. But if they end up going twenty, thirty, forty klicks in, we're going to need a ride. And that changes things." Dawson's comms squawked.

"Zero-One, Control. come in, over."

Dawson held up a finger, cutting off the conversation as he activated his comms. "This is Zero-One. Go ahead, over."

"Zero-One, we have movement in your area approaching from the northwest. Looks like at least a dozen hostiles."

Dawson cursed as he rose and began stripping out of his gear, the others following suit. "Copy that, Control. Any indication they spotted us, over?"

"Negative, Zero-One. No indication. They're spread out. It looks like they're searching for you."

"Understood, Control. We're going to cross the river. We're going radio silent for the next few minutes. Zero-One, out. One-One and Zero-Seven, report to my position immediately, over." Niner and Atlas acknowledged the order and he removed his comms, loading his gear into a waterproof pouch he kept on his utility belt, the others doing the same.

Niner and Atlas joined them a moment later from their covering positions. "What's the plan, BD?" asked Atlas.

"We're heading to the other side. We'll let the current carry us north of the dock, get offshore, and into the trees. Make sure we leave nothing behind. No residual footprint if at all possible—I don't want them knowing we were here."

Dawson sealed his bag and slung it over his shoulders as the new arrivals stripped down. He checked for anything they might have missed, then stepped into the water, the others following. "Time to pretend we're SEALs, boys." He pushed off from the shore. The water was cool but not cold. It actually felt nice. He loved swimming, especially in freshwater. Too many of his ops were in the middle of the desert, and most resorts were by the sea. He rarely hit lake country.

He slowly glided across, gently kicking his legs, not wanting to make any noise, and let the current carry him north of the dock. He reached the other side, pulled himself out of the river, and removed his pack, laying it on the shore. He helped the others out, and they disappeared into the trees then began gearing up.

Dawson fit his comms back in place. "Control, Zero-One. Report, over."

"Zero-One, Control. The patrol is closing in on your former position. Still no indication they know you were there. Recommend you get at least one hundred meters from the shoreline, just in case they've got infrared."

"Copy that, Control. Repositioning now." Dawson rose, indicating for the team to move. He slipped his night vision back into place, lighting up the jungle floor. The last thing he wanted to do was step on a dry stick—the snap might be heard across the river and give them away. "Watch your step, ladies. I wouldn't want anybody breaking a heel. Or a branch."

Atlas' deep voice rumbled. "I think he's talking to you."

"Are you sure?" replied Niner. "I remember you sporting a pair of pumps a few years back on skit night."

Dawson wanted to laugh out loud at the memory but bit his tongue instead. He shushed them, and the conversation fell silent. They continued deeper into the jungle, putting some distance between them, the shore, and the enemy on the opposite side. He breathed a little easier as Langley reported they should be clear. He stood upright, rechecking his gear. "Control, Zero-One. Have you found our road?"

"Affirmative, Zero-One. Right where you said it was."

Dawson smiled. "And just how far does it go?"

"About five klicks due north of the dock."

"Have our little friends made it there yet?"

"Negative. They're about three klicks from your position. They're taking their time."

"Copy that, Control. Give us a bearing."

"Head northeast from your current position. Fifty meters. You should see it."

"Copy that, Control. Heading out now. Zero-One, out." Dawson turned to Niner. "You heard the man. Are you good to make five klicks?"

"I'd rather not, but that's got nothing to do with my near-death experience and everything to do with the fact that I'm lazy. I say we commandeer a ride."

"That could be easier said than done. We don't want to attract any attention to ourselves. We have to get in and out without them knowing we were here."

Niner sighed, heading into the jungle. "Then allow me to take point. If we let Black Conan go first, he's liable to get stuck between two of these trees."

Herrera approached the shore, his ever-present frown creasing his face even deeper. The old man had readily given up where he had sent the Americans. This was no hero, and he was certainly unwilling to die for the cause—or suffer. But he would. He was a dissident. He had already been arrested and taken to the local police headquarters. He would be interrogated, and depending on what ended up happening with the

Americans, he could spend the rest of his life in a small, dark cell. Just like all the others they had already arrested—or would be.

"Search the area. Look for any evidence they were here."

He stared out over the water at the dock on the opposite shore. If he were the Americans, this is where he would come. He would want to see what was happening. They weren't here now, but unless something had interrupted them, they had been here earlier. That meant they saw the boat unload. What they might have gleaned from that, he wasn't sure, but it could mean trouble.

If he were leading the American team, he would want to see where the shipment had been taken. And that meant they would cross the river. He peered at the opposite shore but saw nothing. It was far enough that he didn't expect to. If he were an American soldier, he would probably have night vision gear, infrared, something that would allow him to spot what was on the opposite side of the damn river. But because he was part of the Venezuelan security apparatus, he was lucky to have a radio and a gun. His country was in terrible shape, and it wasn't getting any better. The partnership with the Chinese had to succeed. They needed stability. They needed security. They needed protection from their enemies. And they needed a partner strong enough that they could circumvent the sanctions, sell their oil to a willing consumer, and start replenishing the country's coffers.

They needed this to succeed.

He sighed, turning to one of his men. "Notify the installation to double the guard and activate the jammers. The Americans might be coming."

"Yes, sir."

"And get me a boat. We need to get across the river." He held up his habitual cigar. "I just started this, and I don't intend to swim."

The man chuckled. "Yes, Colonel."

"Oh, and pick up Phoenix and anyone else we saw enter his house. It's time we shut down this cell and find out what they know."

"Right away, Colonel." The man got on his radio, executing the orders.

Herrera turned his attention back to the opposite shore. They had to have been here. Somewhere along here. They would want to get a good view of the boat, to see if they could spot what was being unloaded. And the fact they weren't here now suggested they hadn't gathered the intel they needed.

It wasn't too late to catch them.

Dawson stood at the base of a massive tree, peering up with his night vision gear as Atlas and Spock covered Niner's exploits above their heads.

"Looks like they've got some sort of netting up here," Niner reported over the comms. "I'm taking a sample of it now. Stand by."

The comms crackled, the static heavy, and Dawson gave Rick a puzzled look.

"What's wrong?"

Dawson tapped his ear. "Heavy static on the comms."

"That's not right."

"No, it isn't," agreed Dawson. "Control, Zero-One. Come in, over."

Again, heavy static. And no reply.

"Control, Zero-One. Come in, over."

Nothing. He cursed. "They must have some sort of jammers activated. If they do, they probably have them all up and down the road."

Atlas frowned. "If that's the case, we're incommunicado."

Dawson tried one last time. "Control, Zero-One. Come in, over." Again, nothing but static.

"Coming down now," reported Niner.

Dawson looked up to see the once-dead man scrambling down the massive tree. He dropped to the ground and held up a pizza box-sized piece of the netting.

"This is high-quality shit," he said.

Rick examined it. "This is pricey. Chinese money, not Venezuelan. Expensive as hell. If they ran this the entire route, whatever's at the end of the yellow brick road, they definitely want to keep secret."

"Well, we know there's something there now," said Dawson. "And we know where it is. Now we need to figure out what the hell it is and why the locals think it could change the strategic balance in this hemisphere." He gestured at the netting. "Keep that just in case Washington wants to see it."

"You got it." Niner folded it and stuffed it into one of his pockets. "Comms troubles?"

"Looks that way. We've lost our connection to Langley. Short-range works, but that's about it."

"That suggests it works both ways, doesn't it?" said Niner.

"What do you mean?"

"I mean, if we can't use our comms, they can't use theirs."

"Yes, but they probably have a hardline," interjected Atlas. "Running from the dock to whoever the hell is at the end of the road. They have to have some sort of direct line of communication."

"True," said Niner. "But I was just thinking—they have to send patrols out, right?"

Dawson headed for the road, the others following. "What are you thinking?"

"I'm thinking five kilometers is a long hike. If we intercept a patrol, take them out, we could be there in like ten or fifteen minutes. Long before they'd be missed."

Dawson rejected the idea. "We haven't a clue what's along this road. They could have guard posts, checkpoints, anything."

Atlas reached the road first and pointed up at a device in a nearby tree. "One of the jammers?"

Rick scrambled up the tree then dropped back down. "Chinese. I've seen it before. It's hard-wired with battery backup." He indicated the cable running down the side of the tree. "They're going to have this all the way along here. Even if we cut it, it'll still have hours of jamming capability."

"So, what you're saying is, as long as we're near this road, we have no way to reach home?"

"Exactly."

"Can they still track us?" asked Atlas.

"We already know the answer to that," said Niner. "They were able to track the truck that Rick planted the comms unit on."

Dawson wasn't as quick to agree with that assessment. "Are we sure? I have to assume this is a system that can be turned on or off. Our comms troubles seemed to start all of a sudden."

Rick chewed his cheek for a moment. "You could be right. They might have just enabled it for our benefit. Either way, we're cut off for now."

"What's the range on those things?"

"Not far. A hundred yards in all directions, tops. We wouldn't have to leave the road too far to reestablish communications."

Dawson turned to Spock. "We're gonna advance north on this road. I want you to head northwest. Continue to attempt to make contact with Control. When you do, report our status, get a status on those hostiles, and get them to give you a measurement on how far you are from the road."

"Roger that."

"Let's go, gentlemen," Dawson said, motioning toward the road as Spock set off on his assignment. "Let's keep our eyes and ears open. Rick, you're with me. Atlas, Niner, you're on the opposite side of the road. If they've got this place hard-wired with jammers, I wouldn't put it past them to have cameras as well."

El Consejo, Venezuela

Valeria stared out the window, her heart racing, still uncertain as to what was going on. Her uncle had said they had to get her out of there. Her aunt had rushed her out the back door of the house as her uncle made a phone call. They had followed the fence line of the property all the way to the rear. A few minutes later, a truck had arrived, driven by a man who had been in the house yesterday.

He was a rebel.

"You take care of her," her aunt had said.

"Don't worry. Like she was my own daughter."

Her aunt grabbed her by the cheeks. "I'll tell your mother what's going on."

"What about my father?" asked Valeria, still torn about what she had done.

"He's been arrested," replied the driver. "As soon as things are clear, somebody will get your mother and bring her to you. Now get in the back and keep your head down. There's a blanket there. Get under it."

Tears started flowing, and Valeria hugged her aunt. "I don't want to go."

"You have to, dear. They're after you. They would know you went to the embassy, and that makes you a traitor. You can't stay here anymore. Don't worry, you'll be all right." Her aunt's grip tightened, then she pushed her away. "Now get inside and do everything he says."

"Yes, ma'am." She crawled into the back seat and lay down on the floor, pulling the blanket over her. The engine roared to life, and the truck jolted into gear. They pulled away, leaving her to wonder if she would ever see her home again? Her father, her aunt, her uncle, her friends, her schoolmates? Her town was all she knew, and she was leaving it all behind. She still didn't understand why. Why was this happening?

She needed someone to blame, and the only people she could think of were the man who pretended to be her cousin—and her father, a traitor to his people.

Her shoulders shook as she squeezed her eyes shut, the burn intense. "Where am I going to go?" she asked as they turned onto a road that was a little smoother and quieter.

"If everything goes according to plan? America."

Operations Center 3, CIA Headquarters
Langley, Virginia

"We've lost all tracking," reported Tong as Leroux entered the operations center. He stared at the display showing red dots indicating Bravo Team's locations, as well as the truck Foxglove had tagged. Now, they pulsated rapidly, indicating their last known location, and that active tracking was dead. "Contact Zero-One. Make sure they're okay."

"Yes, sir."

Leroux returned to his station and clasped his hands behind his back as he stared at the screen. All the body cam feeds were dark, as were the binocular feeds providing real-time intel before he had left to update Morrison. Washington was desperate for intel now that the Chinese appeared to be involved, especially with a colonel associated with their hypersonic missile program confirmed in the area. An airstrike was under consideration, but they needed confirmation. It could simply be a mine that the Chinese were financing through their Belt and Road Initiative— a funding program anything but altruistic. Instead, it was designed to provide leverage over governments should the need arise in the future, much like the Chinese-funded ports at either end of the Panama Canal.

Tong turned in her chair to face him. "I can't reach them."

Leroux cursed. "Review the footage. Make sure nothing strange happened just before we lost comms." Out of the corner of his eye, he noticed Packman leaning forward.

"We've got activity at the river," said Packman.

Leroux refocused his attention on the satellite feed, unaffected by what was happening on the ground. It revealed a boat ferrying a portion of the patrol across the river. The cigar-toting man stood at the prow, like a Spanish conquistador of old, lording over all he saw. He reached the dock and jumped off, followed by half a dozen soldiers who rushed ahead. The boat turned back to the opposite shore to collect the rest.

Dawson and his men were about to have company, and there was no way in hell to warn them.

Static crackled over the speakers, and everyone strained to make out what was being said. "—Zero-Five, do you read, over?"

Leroux grabbed his headset and fit it in place. "Control Actual, repeat your last."

"Control, this is Zero-Five. Do you read, over?"

"We read you, Zero-Five," Leroux replied, letting out a sigh of relief at Spock's voice. "What's your status, over?"

"They've got jammers here, running along the road. Short range comms still work, but long range is out. How far away from the road am I?"

There was still a lot of static, but Spock could be clearly heard, and Leroux turned to Tong for an answer. "Approximately fifty meters," she replied.

"You're approximately fifty meters from the road."

"Copy that. That's what I figured. We're heading on foot down the road. It's going to take us about an hour depending upon terrain. We'll be checking in periodically by leaving the road. Anything we need to know, over?"

"Affirmative. The patrol from the opposite side of the river has just crossed. It appears to be led by the cigar-puffing man. Looks like a twelve-man team. There's no way for us to tell if they have vehicles available to them on the other side. Watch your sixes."

"We always do, Control. We'll report back in fifteen mikes."

"Copy that, Zero-Five. Good luck. Control Actual, out."

The steady red dot on the screen showing Spock's position moved to the right then began rapidly pulsating.

"We've lost him again," reported Tong.

"Yeah, but at least now we know what the hell is going on. And if they've got jammers all along that road, there's no way in hell there's something innocent going on at the other end. Any word from Kane yet?"

"Not yet."

Leroux sat. "Then we're just going to have to wait and pray Delta can get there before they're intercepted. We need actual eyes on the target."

"Speaking of eyes," Tong added, "we need ears too."

"Have the New Hampshire deploy a drone. Get it over the area. Let's see if we can break through the jamming. I want to be able to talk to our people more than every fifteen minutes."

South of El Consejo, Venezuela

Herrera stood on the newly constructed dock. He had been appointed head of security for the project months ago. At first, he hadn't been too thrilled. An assignment in the middle of the jungle was not his idea of a good time. But once read in on what was actually happening here, he realized just how important this was and how much faith his superiors had placed in him.

What was going on here was probably the most important thing to have ever happened in this country since the takeover. Chávez had won in a democratic election, then quickly made sure he and his party could never lose again. Many people forgot that today's dictators were yesterday's candidates. Hitler had been elected too. Once in power, he had immediately rid the country of pesky things like democracy. Chávez and Maduro had at least left a pseudo-democracy in place, which, after the last election, was now considered a mistake by their supporters.

Dictators could be elected, even in a democracy. Unfortunately, by the time the people realized their mistake, it was usually too late.

But this project, when it succeeded, would change everything. Complete security. A voice on the world stage. Respect.

Of course, that was his security background talking. This would also be a boon for the people. Economic stability provided by the Chinese in exchange for guaranteed access to Venezuela's oil would mean billions upon billions in revenue for the treasury. It could tame inflation, stabilize the currency, and bring back the economy. No more starvation, riots, or desperate daily hunts for basic necessities.

The dream would finally be a reality.

And full implementation was near, but they couldn't risk the Americans discovering what was going on here until then.

He strode into the canopy of trees overhead and stared up at the artificial camouflage, a digital, three-dimensional canopy provided by the Chinese, effectively fooling any satellite or aerial visual. Out of sight of prying eyes was an entire encampment—fifty soldiers guarding the trailhead, plus dozens of workers and equipment to offload the boats as they arrived.

At least four boats a day had been coming for weeks now. Today, however, had brought the critical shipment. The shipment they had been waiting for. The shipment that would change everything.

He entered a security cabin, where men inside jumped to attention. He grabbed the phone connecting him to the main site.

"Security Site Alpha?"

"This is Colonel Herrera. I have reason to believe that an American Special Forces team is in the area, likely heading your way."

"Yes, sir. We've already doubled our patrols and heightened security, as per your orders."

"Good. Deploy two platoons. Have them head in this direction, sweeping through the trees. We're going to do the same from this side. I want to flush them out, catch them between us. They can't be allowed near the installation."

"Understood, sir. Deploying the patrols now."

He hung up the phone.

"Your instructions, sir?" asked one of the men.

"Wake everyone. I want two platoons sweeping the trees on either side of the road, one hundred meters each side. The first person to spot anything launches a flare."

"And if we find them? Do you want them taken prisoner?"

"No. Just make sure you kill them all."

Dawson continued forward along the side of the road, keeping an eye out for hostiles and any evidence of video surveillance. Niner had gone off ahead, taking point, clearing the way. The guy was remarkable. Less than 24 hours ago, he had been dead. And now here he was, volunteering to put his life on the line.

Everyone had their limits, which was why Dawson had chosen the method he had. Niner wasn't only watching for anyone they might encounter, he too was searching for surveillance equipment. Were there cameras? Where were they? So far, they hadn't seen any evidence of them, and no attempt had been made to hide the jammers. Dawson had the distinct impression the Venezuelans and the Chinese had never expected this location to be found.

"Zero-One, One-One. Come in, over."

Dawson activated his comms, the transmission from Niner loaded with static. "This is Zero-One. Go ahead."

"I'm about half a klick ahead of you. No sign of cameras. You're clear."

"Copy that. Coming to you now. Zero-One, out." Dawson stepped onto the road and indicated for the others to join him. "Let's go. We're clear, but keep your eyes open regardless. Try not to shoot Niner."

"Yeah, we'll never hear the end of it," muttered Atlas.

They broke into a jog. If they had to crawl along either side of the road, they would never get there. But even this was still going to take too long. Langley had said the road ended five kilometers from the dock, and Dawson figured they had covered about two so far. It would take at least another hour if they couldn't use the road. Sending someone ahead on point at a more rapid pace through the jungle saved the team energy collectively, and some time.

Something moved to his left, and Dawson swung his M4 toward the shadow.

"Eagle," came Spock's voice from the dark.

"Talon," responded Dawson, lowering his weapon as Spock joined them on the road. "Report."

Spock glanced behind them. "I had to go out about fifty meters before I finally got a signal. Control reports that our cigar-puffing man and his team have crossed the river. They assume they're coming after us, but they have no way of knowing if they have vehicles available."

"I suspect they do."

"Agreed. We should be expecting company sooner rather than later."

Dawson cursed and picked up the pace. "We need to make better time, gentlemen. Let's get a wiggle on. I want to see what the hell's at the end of this yellow brick road."

Heytea Café

Beijing, China

CIA Operations Officer Dylan Kane sat on the patio of Heytea in downtown Beijing, sipping on his bubble tea with tapioca pearls. It was a beautiful, sunny day with a gentle breeze, but it was spoiled by the incessant traffic and insufferable pollution, though the winds were carrying much of it out of the city today.

He loved it here. He loved the people. He loved China.

It was the government he hated.

Unfortunately, as long as countries like his kept foolishly buying everything the Chinese had to sell, they would continue to fund the war machine China was building. China had 1.4 billion people at its disposal, four times that of America, and with a GDP rapidly catching up to his homeland's, it was only a matter of time before there was a new king of the mountain. Then the world would be at Beijing's mercy, even the United States unable to stop them—unless they wanted to use nuclear weapons. And the Chinese were rapidly building their own arsenal, not subject to the treaties that had focused on the US and USSR.

How many missiles were enough? The estimated 800 warheads the Chinese currently had could certainly destroy America if they wanted, though that was unlikely—why destroy your best customer? But they could definitely be used as a deterrent should they take Taiwan, the South China Sea, or even the Philippines. They had to be stopped before it was too late. Unfortunately, it probably already was. Now all he could do was slow them down.

But today, he was on a side mission, his primary placed on hold. Something was apparently going on in the jungles of Venezuela that Langley believed involved China and hypersonic missiles. If that were the case, this was a big deal. A huge deal. If the Chinese managed to install hypersonic missiles in Venezuela, Washington would be forced to respond—or prove it was willing to relinquish control of its own hemisphere.

What didn't make sense to him was that hypersonic missiles didn't provide much of a strategic advantage. So what if, from the jungles of Venezuela, they could take out a couple of buildings in the US? Yes, that wasn't a good thing, but what would it really accomplish? America's response would be swift, leveling the entire jungle and eliminating any subsequent threat. Even if the Venezuelans and Chinese knew the bombing run was coming and launched all the missiles they had, again, the damage would be minimal in the grand scheme of things.

Hypersonic missiles weren't covered by the Mutually Assured Destruction doctrine. Now, use that hypersonic missile installation to project your power across Central and South America, making it clear you had no intention of ever using it on America unless attacked first—that could be something Washington might sit on their hands for. There were enough problems in the world right now.

Personally, he would still go in and level it. Venezuela was already musing about invading neighboring countries. If they were financed by the Chinese, they might be looking at territorial expansion. Nothing like a good war to distract the population from the problems at home.

The world was ridiculous. He couldn't understand why people just couldn't get along. The problem was there was always somebody else waiting in line. Snap your fingers and eliminate an oligarch, a dictator, or an egomaniac, and there was always someone to replace them. Once Saddam Hussein had been taken out, what happened? It certainly wasn't peace—it was ISIS.

There was always somebody crazier waiting in the wings.

He spotted his contact walking a little too quickly down the street and suppressed a frown. The man should know better by now. Kane took another sip of his tea, savoring the flavor. It was the best he had found in Beijing, though there was a café in Shanghai that was even better. This one he hadn't known about until he mentioned his favorite haunt, and the love of his life, Lee Fang, had revealed this little gem.

His contact sat at a table nearby, nervously fidgeting. A waiter came over and took his order. Kane made certain there was no chance of making eye contact. The man was a nervous wreck. Normally, he was much smoother than this, much calmer. It indicated something was wrong.

And that couldn't be good.

Kane picked up his phone off the table, checking the weather forecast. An indicator in the top-right corner flashed once—the download had been initiated. He flipped over to tomorrow's forecast. More of the same. The indicator flashed again, this time twice. The download was complete.

He flagged the waiter, paid his bill, and left, never once even glancing at his contact. He strolled down the street then climbed into his car, starting the engine. He brought up the downloaded file. It was the personnel file on the colonel they had spotted in the Venezuelan jungle.

And he cursed.

Operations Center 3, CIA Headquarters

Langley, Virginia

"I've got a transmission coming in from Kane," reported Tong.

Leroux hurried to his station. "Send it to me."

"Yes, sir." Tong tapped at her keyboard and the message appeared on his screen before he even reached his chair. "Looks like a personnel file on our colonel."

"How the hell did he manage to get that?"

Tong smirked. "He said, 'Don't ask.'"

Leroux scanned the file, noting that the colonel was currently assigned to hypersonic missiles. He froze then cursed. "Holy shit! Is this right?"

Tong shrugged. "I know we don't want it to be, but Kane says he's confident in the source, though he mentioned the source seemed pretty jumpy, which was out of character."

"That's because he knows damn well what he just stumbled upon." Leroux rose from his chair and hurried toward the door. "Send a copy of that to the Chief. And try to reestablish contact with Bravo Team. We can't wait another hour for them to get there."

"Yes, sir."

He cleared the double doors then jogged down the hallway toward the elevators, finding a crowd. "Make a hole!" he shouted.

Everyone stepped aside, recognizing the urgency. This wasn't some shopping mall. If someone needed to get somewhere fast here, whatever was ruining their day was probably worse than yours if you were simply waiting your turn.

The elevator doors opened, and Leroux stepped inside, hammering the button for Morrison's floor. "Sorry." He held out a hand, blocking the others from entering, and there were no protests. Twice the elevator stopped, but each time, those waiting respected his urgency and stepped back. When he reached Morrison's floor, having saved himself a couple of minutes, he rushed toward the guarded door at the far end of the hall. He showed his ID and placed his hand on the palm scanner. He was buzzed through and was soon in Morrison's outer office.

"I need to see him, ASAP," he gasped, promising to do more cardio.

Morrison's assistant picked up her phone. "Chris Leroux is here to see you, sir. He says it's urgent…Yes, sir." She waved toward the door with a smile as she hung up. "He'll see you now."

Leroux stepped inside, closing the door behind him.

Morrison looked up from his computer, his eyes narrowing. "What's got you so rattled?"

Leroux dropped into a chair. "We just heard from Kane. He got the personnel file for that Chinese colonel from one of his contacts in Beijing. I had it sent to you."

Morrison didn't bother bringing it up. "What did we find out?"

"We confirmed what we already knew—that he's with their hypersonic missile program. And, sir, his previous assignment was with their nuclear program."

Morrison leaned forward. "Go on."

Leroux hesitated, then continued. "Sir, he was specifically transferred to his new position to equip their hypersonic missiles with nuclear warheads." He sat back, his face pale. Hearing the words out loud for the first time was a punch to the gut. "Sir, the Chinese are putting nukes that we have no way to defend against into Venezuela."

South of El Consejo, Venezuela

"Hold position," ordered Atlas over the comms, the big man now on point. Dawson held up a fist, signaling a halt to the advance. Spock and Niner covered their sixes, while Rick remained at his side.

Dawson spotted Atlas rushing back toward their position. "Report."

"There's some sort of checkpoint ahead. Guardhouse with a gate, though it's open. As far as I can see, there are four guards, all inside the security hut. Looks like they're playing a game of cards. They've got a light-armored vehicle. If we got in that thing, we could be there in five or ten minutes."

"Yeah, but then they'd know we're coming." Dawson cursed. "No choice. Let's go around them. We'll take the opportunity to make contact with Langley. Check on the sports scores. See what the weather forecast is for tomorrow."

Niner grinned. "Can I place my dinner order for when we get back?"

Atlas shot him a look. "I thought we agreed we were going to hit the food truck."

"Hey, I'm game as long as I'm not going to hear any bitching and moaning about my gas."

"Dude, just don't get anything with cheese."

"But I like cheese."

Atlas' eyes flared, and his mouth moved as if he were struggling for words. Finally, a fist almost the size of Niner's head appeared.

"See? He knows what I like." Niner grinned as he walked past Atlas and patted him on the cheek. "You had your chance. Angela spanks me now."

Atlas' shoulders slumped. "I can't win."

Rick stared on in disbelief. "And you guys are an elite unit?"

"We've been known to have good days," said Dawson as they headed into the woods.

"Is today one of them?"

Dawson smirked. "The day ain't over yet."

They proceeded northwest, away from the road but still advancing. Atlas pointed ahead then whispered, "The guard post is just over there."

Dawson peered through the trees, spotting some lights. "I see them. Let's give them a wide berth, gentlemen."

As they continued forward, Dawson's comms squawked in his ear. "Zero-One, Control. Do you read, over?"

Dawson activated the comms. "This is Zero-One. Go ahead, Control."

"We're picking you all up. Have you left the jamming area?"

"Affirmative. We're avoiding a guard post. We decided it would be a good chance to make contact."

"Copy that. Stand by for Control Actual."

There was a click, and Leroux's voice replaced Tong's. "Zero-One, Control Actual. We have new intel. Are you in a position to receive, over?"

"Affirmative. We're secure here, over."

"Copy that. We just received the full personnel file on the Chinese colonel you spotted. As previously indicated, he's with their hypersonic missile program. However, we have reliable intel suggesting he was transferred from their nuclear program to outfit their new hypersonic missiles with nuclear warheads."

Everyone froze, exchanging shocked glances. Rick, the only one without comms, looked on, confused. Dawson held up a finger to signal him to wait. "How reliable is that intel?"

"It came from an old friend of yours." Leroux's tone made it obvious he was referring to Kane.

"Understood. What are our orders?"

"We need to confirm if this is true—if they have hypersonic missiles with nuclear warheads on Venezuelan soil, Washington wants to know, and they need to know now."

Dawson cursed. "Copy that, Control. Be advised that we don't have any radiological gear with us. All we can confirm is whether the missiles are there—and even that might be a tall order. We don't know if we're walking in on fifty troops or five hundred."

"Understood, Zero-One. What do you need?"

"We need that radiological gear. Strap it to a damn drone and fly it to our position if you have to. And we're not going to be able to lase any targets with the kind of cover we're seeing. Bring us some beacons. If they've got nukes, we have to take it all out at once. We can't just guess. We need to mark this place."

"Roger that, Zero-One. We'll put together a package and get it out to you ASAP. The New Hampshire is just off the coast. We already have a drone inbound from them. It should be on your location any minute now. We're hoping it'll cut through the jamming. If not, reestablish communications in fifteen mikes, over."

"Roger that, Control. Fifteen mikes. Zero-One, out." Dawson pushed forward. There was no time to waste now.

Rick couldn't hold it in any longer. "What the hell is going on?"

"Our Chinese colonel was apparently transferred from their nuclear program specifically to equip their new hypersonic missiles with nuclear warheads."

Rick's eyes bulged. "Holy shit! If they've got nukes then the rebel intel is far worse than we thought. And if those nukes are active, and we don't take them out all at once…"

"What are we going to do?" asked Niner.

Atlas pointed toward the checkpoint. "There's a LAV over there. We could take out those four guys no problem."

Dawson dismissed the idea. "No, the moment they didn't report in, they'd know. Right now, they still don't know we're here. They think we're here, but they don't know we're here. Langley is going to drop that package for us, then we'll be able to get the proof that we need—that they have nukes on site. Then we need to assess their launch capability. Let's just get our asses to the end of that road as fast as we can." He cut back to the northeast, toward the road. "I hope everyone's been keeping up with their cardio, because this is going to be one hell of a long sprint."

The light armored vehicle advanced slowly down the road that hadn't existed months earlier. Herrera peered ahead into the darkness, his eyes peeled for any signs of motion, but found nothing. The Americans were out there, but he could only move as fast as his troops on foot, stretched out on either side, flushing the enemy forward and hopefully headlong into the troops approaching from the opposite direction. They had to be caught, and they would be caught. He would put an end to this once and for all.

No American would be leaving this jungle alive tonight.

Their secret would be preserved, at least long enough for the deterrent to be in place, so the Americans would never be a threat again.

He peered to the right, out the passenger-side window, watching his men shove their way through the underbrush, inexorably moving forward toward their prey. The Americans were arrogant, almost as arrogant as the Chinese. He was sick and tired of living in a country as good as any other but treated like garbage. All that was needed was for them to be given the opportunity to succeed, to thrive. But because the Americans didn't agree with his country's politics, they were hell-bent on destroying them.

It was disgusting.

Land of the free, my ass.

Free for them? Maybe. But not for anyone who disagreed with them.

He heard something. A motor. His pulse raced. "What was that?"

The driver shrugged. "What was what?"

Herrera rolled down the window and poked his head out, twisting it to the side so his ear was directed upward. Then he heard it—the distinct sound of a drone overhead. He grabbed his radio, pressing the push-to-talk button. "This is Herrera. We've got a drone overhead!" He released the button and heard nothing but static.

"That's not going to work, Colonel. The jammers are active."

Herrera cursed. "Get me to a call box. Now!"

"ETA to the drop?" asked Dawson, the team back on the road. They had to be close. The drone overhead had restored comms, but the connection was still patchy. Static remained heavy due to the jammers, worsening as they neared each one.

"ETA twenty minutes," replied Tong over the comms.

"Copy that, Control. Twenty minutes. Confirm our position, over."

"You're three klicks from the dock, two klicks to go to where we lost the tracking on Foxglove's comms, over."

"Understood. Two klicks to go. Any signs of activity?"

"Indeterminate, Zero-One. The jungle cover is so thick, we can't be sure, but we're picking up intermittent heat signatures to the north and south of your position. It could be search parties. The only reason we picked them up on the other side of the river was due to the trees not being as dense."

Dawson heard something ahead in the distance and held up a fist to signal the team to stop. "Control—"

He was interrupted.

"Zero-One, Control Actual. We've got a launch from the suspected site. It's closing on your position. Take cover immediately!"

Dawson cursed and pointed to his left. "Incoming! Take cover!"

The team sprinted into the trees as the roar of a rocket engine rapidly approached. "Hit the deck!" Dawson ordered as he dove to the ground, covering his head.

How the hell do they know our position?

Operations Center 3, CIA Headquarters

Langley, Virginia

Leroux and his team stared in horror as a missile streaked across the treetops, following the infrared-marked road directly toward Bravo Team's position. Leroux gripped the back of his chair, his knuckles turning white, and cringed as the missile blasted past Bravo Team's position now tracked by the drone. He released his grip, then cursed as the feed from the drone went dark and all the tracking on the team once again disappeared.

"Well, I guess we now know they have defenses," commented Child wryly.

"No shit," replied Packman. "And they've got something to protect."

Leroux agreed. He turned to Tong. "Deploy another drone. Get it in position and land it, if we have to. Warn the drone operators about the defenses. When that delivery gets into position, they're going to have to drop it fast. We can't risk it being blown out of the sky. We don't have time to send another one."

Tong faced him. "Maybe we should send another one now, just in case."

Leroux gave a thumbs-up. "Good thinking. Do it."

South of El Consejo, Venezuela

"Sir, drone is confirmed eliminated. Over."

Herrera had already visually confirmed the report himself, the drone almost directly overhead when it was blown out of the sky via a defensive system provided by the Chinese. Those capabilities were far beyond anything his government could have developed. But if this agreement between his country and China succeeded, defensive weapon systems were only the beginning. Venezuela could protect itself against all its enemies, and, should it desire, expand its territory and increase the natural resources available to it. Venezuela could become a beacon in South America—a military powerhouse.

But only if they could stop the Americans.

The fact the drone had been here confirmed the enemy was as well. There was no way a random drone would be in the sky overhead. The jammers up and down the road were an inconvenience for him but a security necessity. If anybody were to stumble upon what was happening here, any delay in communicating the discovery could preserve their secrecy.

The drone had likely been deployed as a bridge between the Special Forces team and the satellites overhead—the equipment on the UAV was far more powerful than a portable comms unit. The Americans were definitely here, and he had to find them. For this project, for his career, and likely for his life.

If he failed, it could all be over.

Dawson picked himself up and dusted off. He tapped his earpiece, hearing nothing but static. "Well, there goes our comms again."

"Better a robot than us," said Niner.

Spock cocked an eyebrow. "When they take over, I'm telling them you said that."

"I'll deny it to my last breath."

Dawson directed the team back toward the road. "They know we're here. We're going to have to make up some time. Let's dump all unnecessary gear. I want us as light as possible."

Atlas gestured toward Niner hopefully. "All unnecessary gear?"

Dawson shook his head. "No, we're not dumping Niner. Let's hurry up. If they didn't know we were here before, they definitely know now, which means this jungle is going to be crawling within minutes."

Herrera sat in the security checkpoint hut, waiting for the patrol on foot to catch up. This was taking too long. The Americans were here, he was certain of it, and they might have already been encountered, but with the radios jammed, he wouldn't know until they reported in person.

Someone had suggested killing the jammers, but that would be foolish. It would give the Americans free communications with their masters back in Washington. The longer they kept them incommunicado, the better.

He had troops coming in from the north, fanned out on either side of the road, plus his patrols from the south. They would find them. There was no way they were getting through his net.

Herrera spotted one of his men coming through the trees. He stepped out, hailing him. "Did you find them?"

The man shook his head. "Sorry, sir, no. We did find boot prints that seemed fresh. They're definitely here, but it could be Americans, could be dissidents. There's just no way to know for sure, sir."

Herrera dismissed the doubt. "It's definitely Americans. Dissidents don't have drones."

The Oval Office, The White House
Washington, DC

"When will we know?" asked President Hayes, perched on the edge of his desk in the Oval Office. The room was filled with advisors and uniforms, some of whom he was still struggling to remember the names of.

Morrison, his face displayed on a video screen on the opposite side of the room, replied, "The drop is in fifteen minutes. Then they need to get into position, take the readings, get out of the communications dead zone, and transmit. We could be looking at another hour."

Hayes cursed. "Why not just send in a recon plane?"

"If they've properly shielded the warheads, we wouldn't pick up anything, and we'd tip our hand."

Hayes batted his hand dismissively. "They have to know we're there if they shot down our drone."

"Sir, right now, they think we suspect something's going on. We need to let this play out, get definitive proof they have nukes, then respond. If we rush things, we don't know how they'll react."

Hayes folded his arms, not bothering to hide how unhappy he was with how this was playing out. His inclination was to level the entire area and ask questions later, but he couldn't do that. He couldn't attack a sovereign nation without some proof they were up to no good.

Unfortunately, his advisors were right.

"We need proof," said Hayes. "Are you sure a flyby won't work?"

"It would only detect radiation if it was from a poorly shielded source. The Chinese wouldn't be that sloppy. I've been assured those warheads would be heavily shielded, as would the structures they'd be stored in. We would be risking a flight crew for nothing."

Hayes took a breath and straightened up. "Then we wait, but when we have the confirmation, we're all agreed?"

Heads bobbed around the room.

"Very well. As soon as your people confirm what we suspect, I want that entire jungle leveled."

"We could be killing Chinese soldiers. That could be considered a provocation."

"Good. We're not only sending a message to the Venezuelans, we're sending a message to the Chinese as well. Don't put nukes in our backyard. The Chinese are out of control and have been for too long. This time, they're being put in their place. This is our hemisphere, not theirs. It's time to remove them, by force if we have to."

South of El Consejo, Venezuela

Dawson held up a fist and dropped to a knee, tapping his ear then pointing ahead. He had heard something—a snapped branch. Someone or something was approaching. He indicated for the team to break off to the left, leaving the road. They were sitting ducks out here.

They moved into the trees and spread out. Dawson flipped his night vision gear into place, the others doing the same. He spotted a Venezuelan soldier ten yards ahead, creeping through the jungle and peering into the near-complete darkness. The enemy was blind, which suited him just fine. Fair fights were for the movies. Real life meant you took every damn advantage you could.

He drew his knife.

The others followed suit, slinging their assault rifles—except for Niner, who kept his weapon ready, just in case. Dawson waited, his heart pounding a little harder with the excitement of the situation. The target continued to advance, oblivious to Dawson's presence behind the trunk of a large tree. Dawson examined the ground, ensuring he wouldn't step on anything, then readied himself.

The target moved closer.

Five yards.

Three yards.

One yard.

Dawson reached out, clasped his hand over the man's mouth, and slit his throat in one clean, swift motion. He lowered the body silently to the ground and glanced at Atlas, plunging his knife into another enemy's throat. A gurgling sound escaped as Atlas lowered the now-dead man to the jungle floor.

"Eduardo?" someone called out.

The man's voice dripped with fear and revealed his position. Spock advanced rapidly, closing the gap between him and the soldier hiding behind a tree. There was a gasp as Spock disappeared around the trunk, followed by silence.

Three down. How many more were left?

A suppressed Glock fired three times in rapid succession. Dawson's head snapped toward the sound to see Rick standing over a cluster of three bodies, each taken out with a single shot. There had been no way to take three together with a knife—the CIA officer had made the right call.

"Did you hear that?" another voice sounded, speaking Spanish.

"I heard something."

"What was it?"

They were to the left.

Dawson advanced with Atlas, unslinging his M4 and double-checking the suppressor. The voices sounded young, scared—like they didn't want to be here, like they were in over their heads. He spotted them ahead and took a knee, Atlas mimicking him.

"Three, two, one." Dawson squeezed the trigger, taking out the target in his arc as Atlas dropped his own.

Eight down, but there was still no way to know how many were left. All Dawson knew was that they were burning time they didn't have. He signaled for the team to continue its advance. Their opponents were ill-equipped, poorly trained, and only a threat if they weren't careful. Now that they knew the enemy was out there, they could advance cleanly, and with the comms jammed for the enemy as well, there was no way for them to report what was going on.

Something moved to Dawson's right. He turned to see a lone soldier stumbling forward in the dark.

Spock took him out.

Nine.

Unfortunately, nine dead men meant there was no one left to ask how many more of their friends were out there.

They would have to risk it.

"Sir, you've gotta see this!"

"What?" Herrera climbed out of the LAV, flicked on his flashlight, and followed one of his men into the jungle. The soldier led him to a horrific sight. Herrera kneeled beside the body of one of the soldiers sent from the installation. His throat was slit ear to ear, and a large pool of blood surrounded the area, already crawling with insects.

"We've got another one over here!" someone called out.

Herrera growled. "The Americans are here. There's no doubt about it." The efficiency of the kills indicated Special Forces. He pointed back toward the checkpoint and its hardline. "Put the camp on full alert and contact headquarters. We need air support in here now."

He cocked his ear, hearing the faint hum of another drone overhead, and cursed.

Dawson stared up into the jungle canopy but couldn't see the drone overhead. He could, however, hear it clearly. Niner was up in a tree, shining a beacon so the operator could make the drop in the right location. They couldn't risk relying just on their locaters in case the jamming was unexpectedly extended, leaving the drone to drop its precious cargo into enemy hands.

"Zero-One, Control. Releasing now."

Dawson still couldn't see anything. The sound of the drone's engine changed, indicating it had banked away from their position. He heard a crash overhead and spotted something falling through the branches before it got tangled up. Niner climbed down, cut the tangled chute free, and the package tumbled to the ground at Dawson's feet. He unpacked it, handing out beacons designed to mark the target zone, then the Geiger counter and Radiation Isotope Identification Device to Atlas, who slung them over his shoulders.

Dawson smiled, pulling something from the bottom of the package. Candy bars. He held one up. "Someone loves us."

A shout rang out in the distance behind them.

"Somebody heard that. Let's boogie!"

Operations Center 3, CIA Headquarters

Langley, Virginia

Leroux sighed as the trackers on Bravo Team disappeared once again. They had obviously headed back toward the road and into the jamming zone. Moments before, they had confirmed receipt of the package, meaning this mission still had a chance at success.

Morrison entered the operations center, and Leroux stood. "Did they get the package?"

"Yes, sir. Just a couple of minutes ago. They confirmed receipt."

"Good. How far are they from the site?"

"A klick. We'll know soon—assuming they're not walking in on hundreds of troops."

Morrison joined Leroux at the center of the room. "They're trained for it. Hundreds of troops only matter if they know you're there."

"Well, they might not know they're there, but they certainly know they're coming. But like you said, they've done this before. Has the president decided on a response yet?"

"Yes, it's being prepped now. The moment we get confirmation, that jungle is being lit up."

"What about Bravo Team?"

"They'll have to get their asses out of the area before we hit it. The president wants to level the entire site." Morrison tapped his watch. "In minutes, not hours."

South of El Consejo, Venezuela

Herrera held up a hand, bringing his driver to a halt as one of his men ran onto the road, holding something up. Herrera beckoned him over to the passenger side. "What have you got?"

"Looks like some of their gear, sir. We found a bunch of it under some brush. I'm guessing they wanted to lighten their load so they could move faster."

Herrera nodded. "Get to the nearest call box. Tell them to take the site dark." He turned to the driver. "Get me there. They're too far ahead of us to waste time being careful."

Shouts behind them had Dawson and the team sprinting through the jungle. He had decided it was best to stay off the road now, and despite that, they were still making good time. If Langley was right, the site had to be just ahead.

An engine roaring to their right had everyone hitting the deck. Dawson rolled over and peered through the trees to see a light armored vehicle racing past. The distinct flare of a cigar tip brought a smile to his face. "Yo, Rick, is that your friend?"

Rick grinned. "Wouldn't surprise me. If we get the chance, he's mine."

"You're welcome to him. Enough lying down on the job, boys. Let's go."

Dawson scrambled to his feet and advanced. They hadn't encountered any more troops, suggesting they had broken through the search line—likely due to the comms jamming. No one knew reinforcements were needed. They might just make it to their target.

The question was, what the hell were they walking into?

Herrera arrived at the gate, the driver slamming on the brakes and bringing them to a skidding halt. The command to take the site dark had evidently not arrived yet. He cursed, beckoning over a guard. "Take us dark immediately!"

"Yes, Colonel."

The guard rushed off as the gate rose. The driver pulled them into the clearing in the jungle, where the canopy overhead had been replaced by Chinese netting, blocking out the stars and any prying eyes. He had flown over the site himself just a week ago and had been impressed. To the naked eye, the netting appeared perfectly natural. It was amazing what money could accomplish.

He pointed toward one of the domes housing the missiles. "Get me over there, now."

The engine roared as they raced along a dirt road. Across the entire site, lights went dark, the only ones now from flashlights carried by the several dozen guards on patrol, and the dome where the missile systems were being assembled.

There were over 50 troops here, plus scores more support personnel—enough to defend against dissidents with ease. But against a highly trained, well-equipped Special Forces unit, it was another matter entirely.

They needed the deterrent online.

They jerked to a halt in front of the dome, the one structure with lights still blazing out of its open front entrance. It didn't matter. This was the most critical location and nothing could interfere with the work going on inside.

Herrera disembarked and spotted Colonel Chen standing nearby, directing his men.

"What's going on?" asked Chen.

"We think the Americans are here."

Chen frowned. "We're not ready."

Herrera pointed at one of the missile systems. "Without them, we have no deterrent to prevent them from hitting this place. Can you get them online?"

"How long do we have?"

"If we can't stop them from discovering what we're doing, maybe half an hour before they could hit us. Less if they launch from a sub off the coast."

Chen's expression hardened. "Then there's no time to waste."

Dawson reached the edge of the site, emerging from the jungle and hitting the deck, the others spread out on either side of him.

"Well, if we were wondering if something was going on, I think we have our answer," Niner remarked.

Dawson raised his binoculars, scanning from left to right. The flurry of activity was undeniable. At least two dozen guards, most patrolling in pairs, were scattered around the site, armed with AK-103 rifles. One dome-shaped structure stood out—the only one with lights still blazing inside, its double front doors wide open, flooding the area with light.

"What the hell is that?" asked Atlas.

Rick filled them in. "They're launch domes. Used to hide the hypersonic missile system. When you're ready to launch, the top opens."

"Well, it looks like they're trying to prep for launch to me," Spock noted. "Have we seen enough?"

Dawson shook his head. "No. We need to know if these things are nuclear. That changes the equation." He scanned the perimeter, noting what appeared to be an electrified fence. "We need to find a way in. I'm open to suggestions."

Niner pointed upward. "I'll Tarzan in."

Dawson smirked. "Fine. But if I hear a Tarzan call, I'm shooting you myself." He turned to Spock and Atlas. "You two set the beacons on the east and south sides. I want this place lit up so they know exactly where to hit. We can't risk anything being missed."

"Yes, Sergeant."

Dawson rose. "Let's go."

Operations Center 3, CIA Headquarters
Langley, Virginia

Morrison, having stepped out to update the president, returned to the operations center. "Status?"

Leroux gestured toward the main display as he rose. "We're in the dark. Our last contact with Delta was seven minutes ago. They were less than a klick from the suspected site. The security patrol was closing in on them. They don't have much time."

Morrison folded his arms. "What's that famous gut of yours telling you?"

"My gut says they have nukes, but we need proof. A Chinese colonel who might be involved in equipping hypersonic missiles with nuclear warheads being on site doesn't mean there are nukes. He could be inspecting. He could be doing anything. He might have been demoted and sent on a shit assignment."

Morrison grunted. "I don't think we're that lucky. What about those crates?"

"They're the right size, but they were disguised. Generic paneling. There's no way to know without eyes on target. Someone has to open a crate. Someone has to find a warhead and get a Geiger counter close enough to get a reading."

"Don't we have drones that can do this?"

"We do, but the drone we used for the drop had detectors and found nothing."

Morrison cocked an eyebrow, turning away from the screen and staring directly at Leroux. "Nothing?"

Leroux dismissed the concern. "It could just mean they're using good shielding. I wouldn't read anything into it yet."

"All right, keep me posted. We have a massive strike package waiting for your word. The president wants to be able to go to the world and justify why we did what we're about to do. It's all on you."

Leroux groaned. "No pressure."

South of El Consejo, Venezuela

Niner quickly scaled the tree, a little more winded than he should be, concern setting in that perhaps his near-death experience had hit him harder than he thought. Near death. What did that even mean? Had he died? Was he dead? Did it count if it was only for a few minutes?

The fact he had died didn't bother him. He was alive now. But what had been gnawing at him was the fact he hadn't seen anything. There was no bright white light. No angels singing. No cherubs plucking harps while floating on clouds. No Peter at the Pearly Gates.

Nothing.

In fact, he only knew he had been dead for a few minutes because that's what they told him. To him, it was an instant. He died. He was zapped back to life.

Ever since it had happened, he had struggled to remember what exactly had transpired. Was there darkness? Was there nothingness? He honestly couldn't say. He was alive, then he woke up and was told he had been dead.

He planted the beacon near the top of the tree, at the northernmost point of the site. He was about to head down, grabbing a rope to swing over the fence, when he spotted a patrol on foot below. He waited, but they weren't moving, instead taking up position at the base of his tree.

Why this tree, of all the trees?

He stared up at the heavens.

You're just not on my side today, are you?

Then again, he was still alive.

Sorry. Thanks for that.

He pulled his knife, gripping it with both hands, the blade pointed down, and jumped. He silently fell toward the ground, positioning his hands as he did so. The blade pierced the skull of one of the soldiers as he hit the ground, using the now instantly dead target as a cushion to break his fall. He reached up and punched the other in the throat, silencing him, then yanked the knife free and plunged it into the dead man's partner's throat. He gave it a twist then tossed the body aside.

Still got it.

He stared down at his victims. "Sorry, guys. Hopefully, you see the light, cuz I certainly didn't."

He scrambled back up the tree.

Dawson peered through his binoculars, cringing the entire time, then breathed a relieved sigh as Niner climbed back up the tree. "He's clear."

Rick, peering through his own binoculars, shook his head. "That guy's nuts."

"There he goes."

They both watched as Niner swung over the electric fence, dropping to the other side and scrambling behind a prefab building. Dawson aimed his binoculars left to right, searching for any indication Niner had been spotted, but found none.

Good luck, brother.

Atlas' massive frame wasn't built for climbing trees. It wasn't that he didn't have the strength to do it. He could lift this damn tree if he had to. It was that near the top, the branches were thick, and while a little runt like Niner could squiggle through with no problem, Atlas was finding it a little more difficult. He finally reached the top and planted his beacon. From his vantage point, he turned to see Niner swing into the camp on a rope.

He smiled, a Tarzan call echoing in his mind. "That little dude's insane." He scanned the area and cursed. Somebody had spotted him. He unslung his M4 as a soldier rushed toward Niner's position.

Atlas squeezed the trigger. The body hit the dirt, not ten feet from Niner's position. Niner spun, gave a thumbs-up, and dragged the body out of sight.

Atlas continued to scan for others, finding no one else who had taken notice.

Get the job done, brother.

Spock rounded an enormous tree trunk then suppressed a curse as he walked right into a Venezuelan regular taking a piss. Spock reached out and grabbed the surprised man by the head, twisting it sharply. Bones crunched, killing the man instantly. Spock lowered him gently to the ground, then frowned at the sight of the dead man's penis still hanging out. He wasn't about to tuck him in, but the man merited a little bit of dignity.

He rolled him over onto his stomach.

Spock scrambled up the tree, reaching the top, where he planted the eastern beacon. He then took up position with his M4, scanning the area and spotting Niner as he raced toward the suspected hypersonic missile installation.

This plan might just work out after all.

Operations Center 3, CIA Headquarters

Langley, Virginia

"That's the final beacon," reported Tong.

"We now have a perimeter," said Leroux, slapping his hands together as he rose. "Get that data to the Pentagon. Tell them those are the outer markers of the target. Assume a rectangle. Be prepared to hit everything within that area as well as the dock and surrounding area."

"Yes, sir," replied Tong as she fit her headset into place.

Leroux stared at the satellite image. The four distinct beacons, invisible to the naked eye, not only revealed the location of the site, but confirmed that it actually existed. Delta wouldn't place the beacons if there was nothing there to destroy. It turned out Phoenix's intel had been correct after all. Something was happening in the jungle, and the Chinese were involved.

But they still didn't know what the hell was going on.

Were there hypersonic missiles there? Were there nuclear warheads there? And if there were, were the missiles enabled? Were the warheads armed? Were they prepared to launch now, or were they still days away?

The fate of the free world was in his hands, and he had precious little intel to make a decision. Granted, that was rather dramatic—"fate of the free world"—but then again, he was dealing with hypersonic missiles, and if they were nuclear-armed, they could hit Florida in 15 minutes from their current location. They could hit the rest of the continental United States not much later. No, America wouldn't be destroyed in an attack like that. But the resulting war could end all of mankind if it went full nuclear.

The question was, if Bravo Team confirmed nukes were on site and the president delivered his message, what would be the response from the Chinese? He didn't give a shit about the Venezuelan response. It would be like throwing rocks at a tank. But the Chinese had over 800 nukes of their own. Would there be a tit-for-tat response? And if there were, how far would it go? Would they continue to escalate? Could it lead to all-out war?

That indeed could affect the fate of the free world.

He closed his eyes.

Some days, I hate this job.

South of El Consejo, Venezuela

Niner reached the dome structure and took a knee, catching his breath. He quickly scanned the area to make sure no one had seen him, then spun as he heard voices.

Two guards were coming his way from the opposite side.

He readied his knife. He couldn't risk using his gun, even suppressed. Someone might hear him. The guards came into sight, but before he could act, the one on the left hit the ground. Then the one on the right.

Dead.

Someone had his back. He gave a thumbs-up to whomever it was, then headed toward the well-lit entrance of the structure.

And his stomach rumbled. He was hungry and had the trots. Not a good combination while on a mission.

Maybe I should *lay off the cheese.*

But it tasted so damn good. He had always been lactose intolerant, his entire family was, so he had grown up without cheese in his life. But once he had discovered how delicious it was, he couldn't help himself.

Usually, he popped Lactaid to keep it under control, but sometimes it was worth putting up with the cramps just to launch a few air biscuits Atlas' way.

He reached the open side of the dome and swung the Geiger counter into place. He turned it on and cursed as the needle bounced. It could still be background radiation. It could be natural. But he doubted it. He slung the Geiger counter away and pulled out the RIID for a more accurate reading.

And cursed again.

There were definitely nukes inside. The device, designed to pick up trace readings of highly enriched uranium and plutonium, proved what the Geiger counter had picked up wasn't natural.

There were warheads inside.

He snapped his body cam off and held it out, slowly twisting it around the corner to get a shot of what was going on inside.

Someone shouted.

Herrera stood aside, just out of the way, observing as the Chinese crew assembled the missile, prepping it for launch. His own men, here to get trained, stood against the far wall. This wasn't the time to explain how to do things. They needed to be able to launch. They needed that capability so they could warn off the Americans should they strike. Caracas was just waiting for the word. As soon as he could give it, a call would be made to Washington, letting them know that if the Americans launched, so would they.

His heart hammered as the reality of what was going on began settling in. These were nuclear weapons. This was insane. There was no way the Americans would let this stand, even if they were launch capable. He had to think the Americans would still hit the site now that they knew it was here.

Yet, did they know? There was no evidence the Americans had reached the installation yet. He had patrols everywhere. They would have spotted something by now. Then again, maybe the Americans were just here to confirm the location then pull out and let the strike happen—hit the area with everything they had.

But if they could arm this missile, if they could just launch—or at least have the capability of launching—it was still a deterrent. And even if the Americans went through with it, perhaps launching this one missile might make them think twice about launching the next time, if it did hit an American city. If word got out that this wasn't the only site, the entire idea of the deterrent could still work. It could work spectacularly.

He turned to Colonel Chen. "How much longer?"

"Fifteen minutes."

Herrera suppressed the urge to curse as he turned toward the entrance, squinting at something sticking out from the door. "What the hell is that?" His eyes bulged. "Hey!"

Operations Center 3, CIA Headquarters

Langley, Virginia

Leroux's heart raced and his stomach churned as he studied the tactical feed they were monitoring from the Pentagon. The map of the overall area showed naval vessels and submarines steaming rapidly south to join those already in position, not the least of which was the USS George Washington aircraft carrier group, uncharacteristically in the region for a show of force by the new administration. Scores of planes had launched from Florida and Texas, rapidly chewing up the distance and preparing to join those launched from the massive aircraft carrier.

It was awe-inspiring.

It was terrifying.

If this wasn't shock and awe, he didn't know what the hell was.

The Venezuelans didn't stand a chance.

"Holy shit! It looks like World War III," said Child.

Leroux shook his head. "No, but it just might prevent it." He turned to Tong. "Anything yet from Bravo Team?"

"Negative, but the beacons are still in place, suggesting they haven't been discovered."

Leroux returned his attention to America's might on display. "From your lips to God's ears."

South of El Consejo, Venezuela

Herrera pointed at Chen. "Keep working! We need to be able to launch!" He grabbed the hardline, dialing Caracas. "We've been compromised. Americans confirmed on the base." He spotted Chen on his own hardline, saying something in Chinese.

"Beijing is confirming a massive mobilization by the Americans. They're going to hit this site if that Special Forces team gets word out."

Herrera cursed, spinning toward one of the guards. "Equip the pursuit team with jammers. We can't let them get a transmission out."

Atlas sprinted toward the rendezvous position. There was no hiding they were there now, so he continued forward, taking out targets of opportunity on the other side of the fence. The more he eliminated now, the less they had to deal with later.

He spotted an RPG about to be launched toward Dawson's position. He stopped and delivered two rounds. The man dropped, but not before the trigger was squeezed. The rocket launched, flying out of control, finally slamming into the side of a building, a massive explosion erupting as Atlas continued forward.

Secondary explosions followed, causing him to turn and watch an impressive display as what must have been an ammunition depot erupted, the blasts lighting the entire area.

That'll distract them.

Spock sprinted along the tree line of the cleared area and glanced over to see the domed building of interest, its doors still open, lights still blazing inside. He spotted the missile being prepped and stopped. He couldn't pass up the opportunity. He fired half a dozen rounds inside, then continued forward.

Hopefully, his action might delay them, even a minute could prove important. He would love to stick around and hurl more lead, but he didn't have time. They had to get word out about what they had found, and judging from the dozens of troops pouring out of the barracks at the far side of the site, their chances of getting out of here alive were rapidly decreasing.

He pressed forward even harder.

Dawson squeezed the trigger of his M4, removing his target as Rick broke right. Dawson continued to fire, with Rick doing the same, taking down targets as they waited for Spock, Atlas, and Niner to return. He spotted Niner sprinting toward them, an alarm sounding as the compound flooded with light. Dawson triggered the explosives placed earlier, taking out a part of the fence allowing Niner to race through.

Dawson glanced at him. "You good?"

"Peachy. Love the jungle."

"Did you get it?"

Niner tapped his body cam. "I got something, but I don't know what. I did get the readings. Definitely nuclear material here. Probably warheads."

Dawson jerked his thumb over his shoulder. "Get the hell out of here. You need to upload that data to Langley ASAP. We'll hold them off."

"You got it." Niner sprinted into the darkness.

Dawson reloaded then continued to fire, the panicked and disorganized enemy easy pickings.

Operations Center 3, CIA Headquarters
Langley, Virginia

"Whoa, what the hell was that?" cried Child as everyone stared at the screen.

A massive explosion had been caught by the satellite, quickly followed by rapid flashes that showed no signs of abating.

"They must have hit some sort of weapons depot," said Tong. "Looks like secondary explosions."

"Do we have any comms yet?" asked Leroux.

"Negative."

"Where's that drone?"

"Still inbound. This is going to be over before it gets there."

Leroux fit his headset into place. "Get me the Chief. This is going down, now."

South of El Consejo, Venezuela

Herrera picked himself up after the spray of gunfire rattled through the structure. One of the Chinese techs was down, moaning on the floor. Herrera pointed at one of his men. "Get him to the infirmary."

"Yes, sir!"

He turned to the Chinese crew. "Keep working!" He spun back toward his men. "Tell the men to open fire, even if they don't see them. We can't risk them getting their message out. And where the hell's that air support?"

"Inbound now, sir!" shouted someone. "ETA three minutes!"

Three minutes too late.

Dawson breathed a sigh of relief as Atlas reached them, followed moments later by Spock. "Status?"

"Beacon planted," reported Atlas.

"Same," said Spock.

Someone shouted from within the site and gunfire—heavy gunfire—broke out, the enemy finally getting organized.

"Good. Let's get the hell out of here." Dawson turned and sprinted away. The team followed as they tore through the jungle, using the trees as cover. Their job here was done. Hopefully Niner would have the data uploaded at any minute, and the president could make his decision well informed.

Now they just had to save their own asses.

The distinctive sound of RPGs streaking toward them had Dawson cringing, but he kept running. The trees were too thick for the grenades to hit directly. He hoped. He smirked as explosion after explosion behind him confirmed his gamble, tree trunks blasted apart harmlessly. The farther they got, the safer they were.

Dawson activated his comms. "One-One, status?"

"Almost there," came the reply, still filled with static.

Run, little brother!

"Control, One-One. Come in, over." Niner cursed again, as there was nothing but static. He continued to rush forward, desperate to turn back and help his brothers, but those weren't his orders. He had to get the data transmitted. He had to get the video feed uploaded. Otherwise, this was all for nothing. There were nukes here. There were hypersonic missiles here. He had the proof, and Washington needed to know so they could decide what the hell to do about it.

"Control, One-One. Come in, over."

Again, static. But he heard something—a fragment—as he tore through the trees.

"Control, One-One. Come in, over."

"This is Control. We read you, over."

"Stand by, Control. Uploading images now," said Niner as he continued away from the jammers, his body cam in his hand. He pressed the button to activate the uplink to the satellite. The body cam indicated it was transmitting what he had stored. He clipped it back to his chest then swung the Geiger counter around, followed by the RIID, pressing the buttons on both, activating the uploads.

"Control, this is One-One. Uploading now. Confirm receipt, over."

"One-One, Control. Receiving now. What did you find?"

"The missiles are there, and they're nuclear. I repeat, the missiles are there, and they're nuclear."

"Data received. Exfil inbound to Point Alpha. Get your asses out of there, over."

"You don't need to tell me twice. One-One, out."

Niner skidded to a halt then turned, heading back into the fray.

Operations Center 3, CIA Headquarters
Langley, Virginia

Leroux stared at the main display, the video just uploaded from Niner now playing. The Delta Force operator had detached his body cam to reach around the corner of the open door and film what was inside, panning slowly from left to right at what turned out to be a near-perfect angle.

"That's it." Leroux pointed at the missile system being assembled by what appeared to be Chinese troops. "Can you identify that weapon system?"

Tong tapped at her keyboard, the computer mapping the weapon and running it against all known Chinese systems. Within moments, it found a match. "It's a ground launched DF-ZF hypersonic missile system. Shit, we thought these were still in the development stages. It's capable of speeds up to Mach ten, though ground launched might be slower. Still at least Mach five."

Child spun in his chair. "Well, that's one piece of the puzzle confirmed."

Leroux agreed. "What about those troops assembling the weapon? See if they've got any insignia and run their faces. We might get lucky. The more proof we have that the Chinese are actually involved—rather than just Chinese-looking people—the better."

Packman leaned forward. "Look over on the left. Isn't that our Chinese colonel with our Venezuelan cigar puffer?"

"Isolate that segment," instructed Leroux. Tong complied, isolating the best shot they had so far. "Definitely looks like them to me." Leroux turned to the back of the room, where one of the senior analysts, Marc Therrien, had been examining the readings Niner took. "What have you found?"

"The radiological readings confirm the presence of high-grade nuclear material," Therrien replied. "There's no doubt about it. There's at least one nuclear warhead there. Well-shielded, otherwise, these readings would be even higher."

Leroux cursed and picked up his headset, dialing Morrison's office. He was connected immediately. "Sir, Leroux here. We've got the uploads from Delta. It's confirmed, sir. We have video of at least one hypersonic missile system being assembled by what appears to be Chinese technicians. Our Colonel Chen is in the room with them, as well as our Venezuelan cigar puffer."

Morrison cursed. "Do we have any idea how many weapon systems we're dealing with?"

"There's an open crate on the floor that matches what we saw coming off the ship. We witnessed twelve of those being offloaded. We have no way of knowing if there were more already there, but I think we can confidently say there's a dozen weapon systems. And they're nuclear. We have confirmed readings of high-grade nuclear material at that location."

"We have the actual data? We have the proof?"

"Yes, sir. We have the proof."

"And what would your recommendation be, based on what you now know?"

Leroux pinched the bridge of his nose, closing his eyes. What he was about to say could trigger a war. And if it spun out of control, it could be the war to end all wars. "I say go, sir. They're setting up that missile in a hurry, and they're under attack. We don't know if their intention is to launch, but if it is, we may only have minutes."

"Understood. What about Delta? What's their status?"

"We assume they're on their way out of the area, sir, but on foot."

"Well, we can't wait for them. Let's all pray they get clear in time."

South of El Consejo, Venezuela

Dawson spotted Niner rushing toward them. He didn't slow, the sounds of pursuit loud behind him. "Status?"

Niner fell in beside him. "The data has been transmitted. The strike package is probably inbound by now."

"Then let's get the hell out of here and into that damn river. This place is gonna go up like a Christmas tree any minute now."

Niner gave him a look. "What the hell kind of Christmas does your home celebrate?"

Dawson chuckled but said nothing, focusing instead on his footing. One twisted ankle, one broken toe, and it could mean capture. They just had to reach the river, but their pursuers were now firing blindly into the jungle in a desperate attempt to get lucky.

Rick cried out, and Dawson spun to see the CIA officer holding his hand, blood pouring from a wound.

"You good?"

"I'll live. Let's just get the hell out of here."

They continued to run, and Niner added a new worry. "Does anybody know if the river has any piranha?"

Something was shouted by one of the Chinese techs, and Herrera spun to see them all stepping back from the missile system. He turned to Colonel Chen. "Well?"

"It's ready."

Herrera breathed a sigh of relief. "It's about bloody time." He pointed to one of his men. "Open the dome."

"Yes, sir!"

A button was pressed on the wall and the ceiling overhead parted, revealing the netting overhead, lit from underneath by a fire outside.

"Open the netting."

"Yes, sir."

A radio call was made, and within moments, the black mass overhead began rippling, a sliver of stars appearing. The opening widened, revealing more of the night sky. Chen grabbed the hardline and began speaking in Chinese. Herrera picked up his own line, reconnecting with Caracas.

"What's your status, Colonel?"

"We have one hypersonic platform ready, sir. We're ready to launch."

Chen smacked the metal wall of the dome, the sound echoing around the entire curved structure.

Herrera turned to him. "What's wrong?"

"There's a massive strike package inbound. We don't have much time."

Herrera pressed the phone tighter against his ear. "Sir, our Chinese partners are indicating there's a massive strike package inbound. The Americans are going to attack. Contact them and tell them we'll launch if they don't call it off!"

Director Morrison's Office, CIA Headquarters

Langley, Virginia

"The Venezuelans have just reached out. They claim to have hypersonic missiles with nuclear warheads, and they are threatening to launch if we don't call off the strike."

Morrison listened to the update from the Chairman of the Joint Chiefs. He was on a video conference call with the Situation Room, the president sitting at the head of the table, looking harried.

"What do we do?" asked President Hayes.

"Sir, if we don't take them out now, they'll have dozens of them tomorrow, and we'll never be able to take them out. We have to call their bluff. There's no way they'll launch. They know the consequences."

Hayes took a long drink of water. Morrison's years of experience told him it wasn't to quench a thirst—it was to buy time to think. The glass was placed down on the coaster, carefully turned so that the presidential seal faced the man. Another delaying tactic. "Do we know where their president is?"

"Yes, sir," said Morrison, leaning closer to the camera. "We've confirmed he's in the presidential palace."

"Get him on the phone."

"What are you going to tell him?"

"If he launches, I'm nuking Caracas."

South of El Consejo, Venezuela

Dawson sprinted forward, seeing nothing but more damned trees in his way, then smiled as he caught a glint of something ahead. He flipped up his night vision gear and spotted the moon shining off the water. "There's the river! Get in! Swim with the current north. If we get separated, we meet at Point Alpha."

He reached the edge and dove into the water, swimming away from the shore. He turned back, counting the splashes, making certain everyone had made it. The mass of Atlas was last, the splash impressive. Five heads now bobbed in the water, and he started swimming just as the Venezuelans reached the shoreline.

"Get down!" he shouted, then sucked in a deep breath, plunging below the surface as the enemy opened fire.

Operations Center 3, CIA Headquarters

Langley, Virginia

"I see them," shouted Tong, tapping at her keyboard and zooming in on a segment of the satellite feed.

Five bodies were in the water, swimming north. Leroux shot to his feet, checking the map displayed on the right, finding the trackers still dead, indicating the jamming was still in effect. A line of Venezuelan troops on the shore was now firing on them, and Bravo Team disappeared below the water.

"Get that drone back in there," ordered Leroux.

Tong turned. "But it's not armed."

"I know that." Leroux headed for the drone control station. "Have them give me control."

"Sir?"

"Just give me control!" he barked.

Tong flinched, unaccustomed to that tone from him, but there was no time for explanations and second guessing. Leroux sat at the station, the display becoming active, the controls lighting up. "You have control."

Leroux tapped the button to take over from the remote drone operator, orienting himself with the drone's current position and direction. He banked back 180°, rapidly closing the gap with the enemy position now firing on the Delta team.

Hurry up!

South of El Consejo, Venezuela

Dawson held his breath as bullets streaked through the water. Spock cried out behind him, the involuntary reflex muffled. Dawson turned to see his friend struggling and swam back, grabbing him and hauling him to the surface. Dawson gulped in a breath, and Spock did the same before Dawson pulled them both back under the water.

A drone roaring overhead, low to the water, had him pushing his head back up so he could see what was going on. It banked sharply to the left, slamming into the shoreline and exploding. Troops screamed, diving into the water as the fuel on board ignited, spreading out in all directions around the tree line, silencing the gunfire.

He pulled Spock back up, and the man sputtered for air, coughing out the water that had partially flooded his lungs.

"You good?"

"I'll live."

"Excellent. Then you're already one step ahead of Niner."

"I resent that," said Niner to his left.

Dawson did a headcount, relieved to find everyone still alive. They continued to float down the river, the urgency of moments ago now gone.

Now let's just hope they don't send any boats after us.

The phone receiver tightened in Herrera's hand, the plastic creaking in protest as rage consumed him. "What do you mean you're not going to launch? We have to! Otherwise, this was for nothing!"

"It's over, Colonel. Evacuate immediately."

"No, sir! This is our country's only chance! We have to launch! We have to show the Americans that we're done being held down!"

"You have your orders, Colonel. You *will* stand down. You *will* evacuate. This is an order directly from the president and made in consultation with our Chinese partners. They assure us the economic partnership will still be intact."

"Economic prosperity is nothing without security! We can't succeed under the boot of the American oppressor. We have to launch!"

"You have your orders, Colonel. Stand down and evac, or you'll face court-martial."

The line went dead. Herrera slammed the phone down on the receiver, a string of curses erupting that had everyone in the dome— Venezuelan and Chinese alike—staring at him. They had to launch. It was the only way they could show the Americans they meant business. It was the only way to ensure his country's future, its security.

Somebody had to have the guts to do the right thing.

He turned to Chen. "Launch the missile. That's an order."

Chen stared back at him. "You don't have the authorization."

Herrera drew his sidearm and aimed it at Chen. "I don't care. Launch it. That's an order."

"I don't answer to you."

Herrera adjusted his aim and shot one of the Chinese technicians in the chest. The man dropped in a heap, dead. He aimed once again at Chen. "Launch now!"

"No."

He shot another Chinese tech. "Launch, or you're next. We're all going to die anyway. No one will blame you."

Chen again refused. "I will not launch a nuclear weapon against the United States."

Herrera shot the man in the leg. "Launch!"

Chen gripped the wound in his upper thigh, glaring at Herrera as he raised the weapon once again to fire. "No, don't shoot!" Chen hobbled over to the weapon's control system. "Target?"

"The closest major American population center."

Chen worked the controls then stepped back.

Herrera flicked his weapon. "Launch it."

"No. If you want to start a war, you launch it. Green button. Just press it."

Herrera kept his weapon trained on the colonel then stepped over to the platform. He eyed the button, his finger hovering over it. Then he closed his eyes.

May God forgive me.

He pressed the button.

"Oh my God," cried Spock, the first to spot what they all heard.

Dawson spun to see the night sky light up as a hypersonic missile streaked into the air, screaming northward. He activated his comms. "Control, Zero-One. Do you read, over?"

There was a burst of static, the jamming almost clear. "This is Control. We can barely—"

"We have a missile launch! I repeat, we have a hypersonic missile launch! Do you copy?"

More static. The response was unintelligible.

"Why the hell is the jamming still happening? We're nowhere near the road!"

Spock, having taken a round to the shoulder, responded weakly. "They must have portable jammers with them. Someone is still following us in the trees."

Dawson eyed the shoreline but saw no one. "Let's hope the satellite caught that."

Spock pointed at the horizon, contrails streaking toward them, the first elements of the strike package inbound. "Just after the nick of time."

"Heads down!" ordered Dawson as he kicked harder, dragging Spock along as they continued downriver.

Missiles roared past, slamming into the jungle behind them. The entire area lit up as rocket after rocket hammered the site, eliminating any future threat. But it was all too late. A nuclear weapon had been launched.

Somewhere in America, life was changing forever.

Operations Center 3, CIA Headquarters

Langley, Virginia

Leroux watched with satisfaction as Tomahawk cruise missiles launched from the USS New Hampshire, devastated the Venezuelan jungle, leveling everything in sight. Fighter jets reached the coast, missiles launching, detonations indicating the elimination of anti-aircraft missile sites. Airfields were hit, grounded jets erupting into flames, setting the Venezuelan Air Force back into the Zeppelin era.

The Navy and Air Force had already won the day, and it had only taken minutes, the might of the American military on display for the world to see. No one would ever try this again. Of that, Leroux was certain—or at least until another leader came into power who didn't understand history.

"We have a missile launch!" exclaimed Tong.

Leroux spun toward her immediately. "Confirm your last!"

Tong pointed at a display showing a target moving rapidly north. "We have a missile launch. It came out of the site just before we hit it."

"What's the target?"

"Unknown. Too early to tell. It's currently bearing three-two-zero degrees."

"Plot the possible destination."

She tapped at her keyboard, a dotted line extending northward from the tracked missile.

And the entire room stopped as she zoomed in on Florida.

"Miami," her voice cracked.

"ETA?"

"Fifteen minutes."

Leroux's heart hammered. "Notify the Situation Room."

"Can we stop it?" asked Child, the horror in his voice obvious.

Leroux shook his head. "It's hypersonic. Only if we get lucky."

Director Morrison's Office, CIA Headquarters

Langley, Virginia

Morrison read the flash message on his screen from Leroux's team, then cursed out loud.

Hayes looked up. "You have something to add, Leif?"

"Sorry, Mr. President, but we have an inbound hypersonic missile launched from the site."

The room erupted in activity, every phone on the boardroom table grabbed.

"Is it nuclear?" asked someone.

"We can't know, but we have to assume so."

"Do we know the target?"

"Initial tracking suggests Miami."

Gasps filled the room.

"Projected damage. How many people are we talking about?" asked Hayes.

Morrison gripped the arms of his chair. "It depends on the size of the warhead. It's most likely a tactical nuke. They're meant for the battlefield. But on a city? It all depends on the yield. If we assume something the size of what we used on Hiroshima—fifty to seventy-thousand dead in the initial blast, at least as many injured. Not to mention the long-term consequences depending on fallout, wind directions—there's just no way to know. The death toll will be massive. If it's a fifty-kiloton yield, we could be looking at hundreds of thousands dead."

"Can we stop it?"

The Chairman of the Joint Chiefs leaned forward. "We're going to throw everything we have at it, sir, and hope for the best. But this is a hypersonic missile. Shooting them out of the sky would be a fluke."

"Can we evacuate?"

"No, Mr. President, there's no time, and we don't know where exactly it's going to hit. We could kill more than we save."

Silence fell over the room.

"I will *not* be the president that didn't give American citizens a chance to save themselves. Issue the alert."

South of El Consejo, Venezuela

Dawson continued to swim downriver as the unrelenting pounding carried on nonstop behind them, leveling the missile site. Fighter bombers flew overhead unchallenged as they continued to deliver a message to both the Chinese and the Venezuelans.

Don't mess with America.

From his vantage point, he could tell that not only had the immediate area they had marked with beacons been decimated, but so had the area near the newly constructed dock. In fact, it appeared they had hit the entire road. If they had, it likely meant their Chinese colonel and the cigar-puffing Venezuelan were dead.

He took great satisfaction in that.

He glanced over at Rick, bobbing in the water nearby. "Sorry you didn't get your shot at Cigar Boy."

Rick grunted. "No worries. I'm pretty sure he's toast."

"Almost definitely."

Spock gasped, and Dawson spun around to see Niner tying off the wounded warrior's arm.

"You alive, brother?"

Spock squeezed his arm and winced as Niner held him, helping him stay above water. "Yeah, but how many are going to die because we failed?"

Dawson frowned. It was a good question. They had comms now, and apparently the missile—the one they had seen launch—was heading for Miami. They had no idea how many kilotons the warhead was. But in order for it to be an effective deterrent, he was certain it was a reasonably sized tactical nuke. Hiroshima had been 15 kilotons. A lot of tactical nukes today were 50 kilotons.

Briefings he had received in the past indicated that something like that, detonated in a city core, could kill 100,000 to 200,000 instantly, with a similar number suffering burns and other horrific afflictions. And then there was the radiation. It could make hundreds of thousands more sick, with people dying for decades afterward from cancer and other ailments.

They had failed to prevent the launch—though that was never their mission. Their mission was merely to confirm what was there. He had no doubt the missile had been launched because the strike had been ordered. If Washington had waited and instead used diplomacy to remove the missiles, then Miami wouldn't be in danger. Yet he understood the impulse. Swift action. Limited damage. Level the area.

Send a message, and it's over.

He was quite certain nobody ever thought—nobody ever dreamed—the Venezuelans would actually launch. In fact, it was so outrageous that he had to assume it was a rogue launch, something done against orders, because if Miami was destroyed, the response would send Venezuela back into the dark ages.

And God only knew what would happen with China.

It could mean World War III.

He sighed. They should have destroyed the installation themselves as soon as they confirmed the nukes were there. But that, too, would have been against orders.

No matter who was to blame, he would live with the guilt for the rest of his life.

Operations Center 3, CIA Headquarters
Langley, Virginia

Leroux stood, his hands clasped behind his head as he stared in disbelief at the tapped-into Pentagon tactical feed. Scores of missiles were in the air—aircraft launching from every southern air base, helicopters, drones—everything, all in a desperate attempt to halt Armageddon.

A news alert scrolled on one of the displays, selected headlines shown. He snapped his fingers. "Put CNN up."

A screen opened, showing the news network with a red chyron at the bottom: MISSILE INBOUND. MIAMI RESIDENTS ORDERED TO SEEK SHELTER.

"Holy shit!" gasped Child.

A CNN camera crew, shooting from a rooftop, showed residents staring up, their phones in hand, disbelief etched on their faces as the emergency alert blared en masse.

The panic was near-instantaneous.

"I can't believe this is happening. Not in America," murmured Packman,

"My brother is in Miami!" gasped Child.

Packman wheeled his chair over and gave the young man a hug. Child burst into tears, sobbing uncontrollably. Then he broke free, grabbed his phone, and dialed, pressing it to his ear.

"Hey, bro, it's me…Yes, it's real." His voice cracked. "Just get underground if you can…I-I love you too. I'm so sorry I didn't call you more often, I didn't make more of an effort. Oh God, I'm so sorry!"

Tong whimpered and started crying, and Leroux collapsed into his seat. They had failed.

The blood of hundreds of thousands, if not millions, would be on their hands. For this was just the beginning. If Miami was hit, retaliation would be demanded. They could be witnessing the start of World War III.

And it was his fault.

South of El Consejo, Venezuela

"There they are!" said Niner, pointing ahead.

Dawson sat up, treading water, and spotted the Black Hawk and its escorts on the horizon, thundering toward them. The aerial assault behind them was now finished, the jungle glowing with the aftermath. The pilot expertly guided the massive airframe into a hover just above the water. Spock was hauled up first, the flight crew helping him in, then Rick with his wounded hand. Niner and Dawson pushed the big man, Atlas, over the edge before climbing in themselves.

"All clear!" shouted a crewman.

The pilot banked away, heading back to America, heading back to freedom, heading back to God knows what.

Dawson activated his comms. "Control, Zero-One. Do you read, over?"

Tong's subdued voice replied, "Affirmative, Zero-One. We read you, over."

"Status on that missile?"

There was a pause, and he heard a sniff. She was crying. "Still inbound."

"Have we confirmed the target?"

"We still believe it's Miami."

"Can you stop it?"

"We-we don't know. We're launching everything we've got at it, but it just hit Mach five. It's like shooting a bullet with a bullet."

"They have to try!" said Dawson uselessly.

"You don't think we know that?" She gasped. "I'm so sorry."

"It's not your fault. It's our fault they spotted us inside the wire."

Leroux's voice cut in. "This is Control Actual. Bravo Team, it's not your fault. It's mine. This was my mission, my call. I recommended the strike proceed."

"Bullshit," said Niner, cutting in. "I got spotted. It's my fault. If I had been more careful, they never would have known we were there."

Rick, now equipped with comms, held up a hand. "Listen up. It's nobody's fault but the enemy's. It's China's fault, and it's Venezuela's fault. It's whoever gave the order to put those missiles in there. It's whoever got the idea in the first place. It's not yours. It's not ours. We did everything we could to stop this."

"He's right," Dawson inhaled deeply. "Does anyone have family in Miami?"

Atlas buried his head between his knees. "My sister's there, visiting a friend. She has her kids with her."

Niner slid over and wrapped an arm around the big man's shoulders. "Call her."

Leroux cut in. "Give me the number. I'll patch you through."

Miami, Florida

Larissa Williams leaned against a light pole, her three sons held tight against her as tears flowed down their cheeks. Her entire body trembled in terror. She didn't know what to do. She didn't know where to go. This wasn't her city. This wasn't her home. She wasn't supposed to be here. She wasn't supposed to die today.

People were running in all directions—screaming, crying. Some stood in stunned silence. Some appeared to know exactly where they needed to be, but most were running around in shocked confusion.

She had received the alert inside a movie theater, the boys begging to see the latest superhero nonsense. Her friend had dropped them in front of the multiplex, begging off going with them, using the need to pick up groceries as an excuse. The alert had been terrifying, like something out of a movie. One minute, they were watching a movie, laughing and happy. The next minute, every phone within earshot emitted that terrifying, ear-piercing warning.

When she first read the alert, she thought it was a joke. A mistake, like what had happened in Hawaii a few years back. But a second confirmation came moments later.

It was real.

Then the world went crazy.

She had grabbed the children and gotten them out of the theater as people immediately lost all concern for their fellow man. Instead, they thought only of themselves. People were knocked down, people were trampled, and when they emerged, there was gridlock on the streets, cars slamming into each other as drivers jockeyed for position, desperate to get out of the city.

But there was no time. The alert had said 12 minutes.

How the hell could you get out of a city like this in 12 minutes?

Her phone vibrated in her hand, and she flinched, almost throwing it away in fright. She stared at the display, but she couldn't make it out. Wiping her eyes dry, she cried out in relief.

It was her brother.

He would know what to do.

She took the call and pressed the phone tight to her ear, the surrounding noise almost deafening. "Leon, is that you?"

"Yes, sis, it's me. Where are you?"

"Oh God, I'm in Miami!"

"I know, sis. Where in Miami?"

"I don't know—downtown. I don't know what to do. I have the boys with me. I don't know what to do! Tell me what to do!"

"Do you see any police officers?"

She wiped her eyes dry again and looked around her. She spotted two on a nearby corner. They were directing people into a nearby office tower. "Yes, I see two on the other side of the street."

"All right. Go to them. Ask them where to go. They should have a disaster plan that's being implemented. But you need to get underground. Get into an underground parking lot, somewhere, anywhere with a basement. Just get underground."

A siren erupted—some sort of air-raid-type warning. It sounded like something out of a movie about the London Blitz. A car sped up onto the sidewalk, slamming into several people before it came to a halt. The driver was hauled out and pummeled mercilessly.

She covered the boys' eyes. "We're gonna die! We're gonna die!"

"Just go to the police! Do you hear me? Go to the police!"

"I can't! It's just too much! There's too much happening! What are we gonna do? Is it really happening? Are you sure it's happening?"

"Yes, it is. I wish I could tell you something different, but it is."

Suddenly, everything fell quiet. The world around her faded as reality set in. "We're gonna die, aren't we?" she said, her voice calm, the panic gone.

"I don't know. We're doing everything we can to stop it, but I just don't know."

"Are you involved?"

And then she heard something she had never heard in her life—her brother was crying. "I'm sorry. I should have tried harder. Can you ever forgive me? Please forgive me!"

The call cut off as planes streaked overhead.

Her youngest son stared up at her. "Mommy, are we gonna die?"

The world came rushing back—the panic, the terror, the horror, the chaos.

"No, baby. No, baby." She hauled him into her arms, then took the others by the hand, a sudden determination to survive taking control.

There was no way she was dying without letting her brother know there was nothing to forgive.

Operations Center 3, CIA Headquarters

Langley, Virginia

"My God, I don't think I've ever seen anything move that fast," said Therrien from the back of the room. "I'm showing Mach five."

"It's incredible," agreed Packman.

"Well, if we ever wondered if the Chinese had the capability, we certainly have our answer now," said Leroux. "ETA?"

"Six minutes," reported Tong.

Child continued to sob, his phone call with his brother having been cut off, the cellphone system overwhelmed. To the young man's credit, he was manning his station once again. Most of the room was on their feet, staring at the screen, more news stations now showing, all reporting the horrors of uncontrolled panic.

They were witnessing something that should never be witnessed—the final moments of so many innocents.

Leroux couldn't help but wonder if warning them had been the right thing to do. Was it better to be like Hiroshima, where your day was peaceful one moment and over the next? Or was it better, over those few minutes, to say goodbye to a loved one?

All the screens suddenly switched to the presidential seal, then the man himself appeared from behind the Oval Office desk.

Leroux snapped his fingers. "Give us audio."

Tong tapped at her keyboard, and the presidential address sounded.

"My fellow Americans, our country faces a great tragedy. At this moment, a hypersonic missile is en route. We believe Miami is the target. We have reliable intelligence that it is armed with a nuclear warhead. It was launched from a Venezuelan facility but is a Chinese weapon. We have proof that the Chinese brought in the weapons, equipped them with nuclear warheads, and facilitated the launch.

"For those of you within the sound of my voice, for those about to die, for those about to lose loved ones, hear me now—you will be avenged. And to the Venezuelan government and the Chinese dictatorship, I swear, if that missile detonates on American soil, those responsible will die. Every single last one of you."

Over International Waters

North of Venezuela

"Holy shit! Did he just declare war on China?" exclaimed Spock, all of them listening in through their comms, Langley having patched in the address.

"I don't know. I hope not," said Niner. "I've got plans this weekend."

Rick stared at him incredulously. "Really? You're joking now?"

Niner shrugged. "It's what I do. It's my coping mechanism." He reached out then wrapped both arms around his best friend, still silently sobbing. The big man didn't protest, instead returning the embrace.

And Dawson stared up at the heavens.

Please, God, save us from ourselves.

Operations Center 3, CIA Headquarters

Langley, Virginia

"The USS George Washington just spotted it," said Tong, bringing up a feed from the naval vessel.

Leroux stood as the contrail from the missile streaked across the sky at incredible speed.

"My God!" gasped Packman.

Suddenly, there was an explosion on the horizon, massive, a mushroom cloud erupting into the night sky.

"Tell me that wasn't Miami," murmured Leroux.

Tong faced him, jubilation on her face. "No! It detonated at least two-hundred miles short of the coast, over international waters!"

Cheers erupted, and Leroux collapsed into his chair as hugs, kisses, and high-fives broke out all around him. He fit his headset in place, dialing Morrison. "Sir, are you seeing what we're seeing?"

"Yes!" confirmed an excited Morrison.

"Do we know what happened?"

"Negative. Stand by. The president is getting calls from both the Chinese and Venezuelan presidents. What's the status on our team?"

"They're over international waters. Two wounded, including our officer, but they're safe. And so are all of us, apparently."

"Good work, son. Damn good work."

Infirmary

USS George Washington

Dawson stood at the foot of Spock's bed in the infirmary on board the USS George Washington. Rick was in the next bed, with Niner and Atlas standing nearby.

"So, what's the word?" asked Spock, his arm now properly bandaged.

Dawson, having just come from a secure comms room after a briefing by Clancy, shook his head. "Who the hell knows what the actual truth is? The Venezuelans claim it was a rogue colonel who ordered the launch. And the Chinese claim that all unauthorized launches were pre-programmed to ditch if they weren't aborted, and detonate so the weapon couldn't be retrieved by hostile powers. Apparently, they never intended to allow the Venezuelans to have the actual capability of launching a nuke."

"Sounds like bullshit to me," said Atlas.

"Bullshit's got my vote too," seconded Spock. "But I guess it doesn't really matter. The threat's been eliminated."

"And other than the entire state of Florida collectively shitting their pants, we're none the worse for wear," rumbled Atlas.

Niner snorted. "Look who's got his sense of humor back."

Atlas shrugged. "My sister's fine. So are the boys." He turned to Dawson. "I think we deserve a few days off, don't you?"

"I do, and so does the colonel. After we debrief, he's giving us a week off. Now that we're not going to war."

"Good. I want to help Vanessa with her food truck. Apparently, she's a hit and is getting swamped."

"That reminds me." Dawson walked over to Niner then belted him in the shoulder, hard, knocking him off his feet. "I told you one day I'd hit you and you wouldn't know it was coming." He jabbed a finger at the downed warrior. "My wife does *not* have balls."

"Lady balls!"

John F. Kennedy International Airport

New York City, New York

Valeria descended the escalator, gripping her mother's hand tightly. It had taken a week for her to join her in Columbia. The American embassy had been contacted, and they had received instructions to report there. It was another week before arrangements were made for them to fly to America, and now they were here, landing in New York City.

Her heart pounded with excitement. She was here, finally in America, her dream coming true.

But it also broke her heart to leave everything behind. Her father and brothers had been arrested. So had her uncle. So had many of her neighbors and friends. But she was alive. Her mother was alive. And maybe, someday, with people like her uncle continuing to fight, her country would be free again, those unjustly imprisoned would be released, and Venezuela could once again thrive like it had before.

They reached the bottom of the steps, and their escort—an American woman they had just met coming off the flight—guided them to the left. "There's someone here who wants to meet you."

A young man stood there, smiling. Her mother gasped, rushing forward, her arms extended. "Oh my God! Diego, is that you?"

Valeria's jaw dropped as she realized this was the real Diego, her real cousin.

Her mother embraced the man, then stepped back. "Valeria, this is your cousin Diego."

He smiled at her, then held out both hands—a small KitKat in one, a Reese's Peanut Butter Cup in the other. "A friend of yours told me these were your favorite."

She smiled and rushed into his arms, hugging him tightly as he laughed, returning the hug.

"Welcome to America."

THE END

ACKNOWLEDGMENTS

When I killed Niner, I debated leaving him dead, then decided against it. There'd be a lynch mob outside my door before the end of release day. I've come to love these characters, as many of you have, and consider them family. When I do kill a recurring character, it is never easy, and yes, tears are shed.

With my own mortality in question, I've debated putting together a final goodbye, where I run down the major characters and say where I see them ending up. As I think of it, tears fill my eyes because I don't see all of them making it, and it's also sad that my head is in that space.

Life can suck sometimes, but I'm fortunate that I'm not alone.

I might do that "How it ends" missive, with instructions to publish it when I pass, and if I'm lucky, it will be my grandchildren posting it, and not my daughter.

I haven't given up hope just yet.

There's just too damned much to live for, too many stories left to write, too much love left in me to not share.

Great-grandchildren?

As usual, there are people to thank. My dad for all the research, Alex Enright for the torture music example, Brent Richards for some weapons info, Mimi Dunski for the Atlas Burger suggestion, Stephen Mcivor for inspiring Vanessa's food truck name, and, as always, my family and friends for their continued support, my late mother who will always be an angel on my shoulder as I write, and my fantastic proofreading team!

To those who have not already done so, please visit my website at www.jrobertkennedy.com, then sign up for the Insider's Club to be notified of new book releases. Your email address will never be shared or sold.

Thank you once again for reading.